I0553435

Writer's Block Publications

And

The Lyricist Firm

Presents

Peek-A-Boo

{The Safe Deposit Box}

By

Veronica Meek

&

Mike Sudler

Writer's Block Publications
P.O. Box 640
Jonesboro, GA 30237

This is a work of fiction⋯ Names, characters, places, and incidents are products of the author or author's imagination. No part of this book should be reproduced in any form or by any means without written consent from the Publisher.

ISBN-13: 978-0615760834

ISBN-10: 061576083X

Editor-Kiara Reynolds

Cover Design by The Lyricist Firm

Manufactured in the United States of America

Author's Bio

Veronica Meek

I'm the oldest of 5 kids and maybe the only one that loves to write. I am a mother of 3 and I love to share most of my writing with them because I want them to see me follow my dream through so they feel like if mommy can do it then so can I. With them being so into what I do with my writing I try to touch all bases and write in all areas so all adults and children can read me.

I'm proud to say that I am member of *The Lyricist Firm* and also *The Firm Divas*. I joined those groups because they take their writing seriously just as I do. I have been writing for about 5 years off and on, but lately I have been doing it full time. I am a poet in heart just as well in mind. I lay all of my soul out for the world to read and hopefully someone would listen and understand that they're not along in this sometimes cold world.

I have also started my own publishing company *Writer's Block Publications* that is home to a few new authors that are also determine to make something wonderful out of their hard work. So I would like to take time to say THANK YOU to a few of my writers that would have book coming out sometime this year *Quameek Kaleph, Meldamion Huguley, and Keshawn Jones.*

I also have a book out already under called The Hitman's Daughters.

Thank you... Atlantamoody

Author's Bio

Mike Sudler

A Poet, A Writer, A Story Teller, putting my thoughts together and producing books for the reader's enjoyment. I am an Official Member of *"TLF"*, and give my all to *"The Fam"* to bring you the best we have to offer. I don't really have any particular writing expertise; I just express what I feel at the moment...

I started out writing back in 2000 doing odd pieces for a few people, poems for anniversaries, birthdays, and various holidays. When I wasn't doing that I wrote pieces for myself. Being heartbroken at that time, I wrote love poems. After about a year and a half I started doing Christian Poetry...

Realizing that I had a knack for writing I took it to a website and started blogging my views. I have since come across quite a few talented writers of the pen, and thus *"TLF"* was formed. It wasn't I who gave it the name or it's full start, but I was co-writer with the many people who have had their Firm days. Now, I am Owner/Operator of *The Lyricist Firm LLC*...

After a year of trials & tribulations. We have started accomplishing our goal. With 4 books out now and my solo lyrical style book, we are well on our way to growing toward a future of becoming a ground breaking company opening doors into the world of writing, leading many talented individuals toward their dream. I only ask that you please give us your support.

Thank you... PWP

Chapter 1

Greg

The rain is coming down hard tonight. I love it when it storms, because rain always puts me in a sexual mood, the one thing I hate about being along is the fact that I have no one to share my rainy nights with. I stand in front of my balcony window just staring into other condos. It has become something of a habit for me watching to see what's going on in the other apartments. I looked down at my watch knowing it was about time for her to come home. She's more like me then she knows because her nights are as lonely as mine. And like clockwork she opens up her apartment door and I can tell that she is soaking wet. Her cloths are sticking to her body like a second skin.

I walk out on my balcony because I love to watch her. There is something about her that turns me on. Her apartment is dark except for the front. I think she has a motion detector because the come on as soon as she opens the door. It's still kind of warm outside and the fact that her clothes are stuck to her, doesn't seem to matter. She stands there going through her mail, while water is running down into her beautiful face. I love that from where I'm standing I can see inside of her entire apartment. I shut the door, take a seat, and close my eyes for a moment listening to the storm working its magic.

When I open my eyes again she is in her bedroom and has turned on the lamp beside her bed. Man was I happy; I opened my eyes in just the nick of time. She starts to remove her shirt. I sit up in my chair with my back straight and my manhood jumps to attention. It is like I have been waiting all day for this. I have to move my man down a little bit as he starts pushing up hard against my jeans. My hand cuffs my muscle and I give it a little squeeze so he can behave just a little while longer. The cover of darkness covers me so I decide to unbutton my pants to give myself a little more breathing room. It's hard trying to keep my 10 inches down. He is begging to be set free.

She takes that moment to walk in front of her window, the soft light glowing off her half naked body. I rub myself up and down as she reaches behind her and unbuttons her bra. My month opens as her bra falls down to the floor. Her breasts sit up nice and I just want to reach out and touch them. I watch as she steps out of her pants. She removes them slowly as if she knows I am watching her. And as if she has been reading my mind, she looks up at me and smiles.

Susan

It's around 9'ish, the time I usually get in from the office. I hadn't expected the rain tonight, and as hard as it was coming down, traffic was light. I drove into the garage rather than park out on the street, being already soaked; I just figure I can spare myself the extra wetness. And it was closer to the mailbox. It's been a month since Tom had left for Iraq, and I haven't heard from him at all. I suppose the many nights he spent laid up with me, wasn't half the love he had for his wife and kids. It doesn't matter because just like a puppy love school girl, I check the mail faithfully every day. As I enter my humble abode, I shuffle through the new postal delivery of bills and an invitation to this year's Black-tie VIP Dinner for the top Executives at The Law Firm. Nothing from Tom... again! Now to get out of these wet clothes, and into a hot bath.

From one room to another, blouse, bra, skirt... into the bathroom to run my water, but first I walk over to the patio glass doors, one hand on the handle to slide it open. If it wasn't for so much rain, it would've been such a beautiful evening. On the other hand the rain however, made it a romantic setting. The nights I shared with Tom on the balcony in the rain... ohhhh how I long for his passion. Reminiscing about being draped over the balcony, with his masculine frame of a man behind me, holding me ever so gently. Hislarge hands covering my always erect breasts and his manhood deep inside the warmth of my wet Susie. *(That's the name he gave it.)*. Stand there in the archway I slide my panties down, and slightly massage my shaven Susie with two fingers. I'm so wet and deeply horny.

I hear Tom's voice in the back of my mind. "Is Susan going give me some wet Susie?" I smile; and am about to turn and go for my relaxation time when I glance out and see someone looking over. I turn with an even bigger smile, and head toward my bath.

Chapter 2

Greg

I watch as she turns and walks away. Now that is a woman after my own heart. She knew I was watching her and her smile was breath taking. What I wouldn't do to get to know her. I.ve been single for too long for me to have to stoop to the level of a peeking tom, but I can't help it. She turns me on in the worst way. I can tell from her reaction that she is missing the touch on a man and I'm damn sure missing the touch of a woman. I reach down and touch my man again, this time I pull him out.

The mist from the air is hitting him and I close my eyes once again thinking about her tongue licking across my head. I feel myself harden even more as the rain, a warm mist fall down lightly on me. I start having flashes of the sexy lady kneeling down in front of me.She looks up at me with soft brown eyes and smiles. Then she reaches down and grabs my man in her hands. I watch as she lowers her head and wraps her lips around me. It is easy for me to keep the fantasy going with the warm mist hitting me more and more.

I move my hands slowly up and down my hardened man and he is jumping up for my touch. My eyes are closed as I picture myself lowering her head down until she starts to deep throat me. The storm around me is getting harder and lightning starts flashing across the dark sky lighting up my whole balcony as soon as I open my eyes again. I feel like someone is watching me and when that lightning lights up the night. I know they got a very good look at what was happening on my balcony.

Susan

I sigh and let out a gasp of air in relief. Shutting my eyes, I can almost see the face of "HIM". Not Tom, this is awkward... to a point exciting. I find myself being turned on. I flip the switch to keep the water heated, and produce more bubbles. Leaning my head back, exhaustion takes over and I slightly nod off, thinking about "HIM" again. My legs open and my hand go down between them. I see "HIM", standing there in the threshold of my bathroom doorway. He's wearing a bathrobe. One that I had gotten Tom for his birthday last year... he never wore it, we were always nude.

I feel myself slide down a little more into the water as I raise one leg over the top of the tub and the other leg over the other side. Now I'm open wide enough to rub myself with two fingers, with ease. Massaging my pearl up and down, switching to a circular motion, then up and down again. He walks over to me, and releases his robe. I watch it drop to the floor and slowly look back up to his already hard *"I want to fuck you"* erection. He steps into the tub.

Now I'm rubbing myself vigorously, he pauses in front of me and looks down. I reach up and take his Mandingo into my hand, and slowly wipe my tongue across the head. Lifting it up, I lick down his long hard shaft, and then back up.

Then opening my mouth wide to receive his pulsating head, and I suck. I found myself slightly teasing it a bit. I go down the shaft with my tongue again, now inserting more of his pussy poker into my mouth, down my throat. His legs tremble a little. I reach up and cuff his balls. He reaches down grabbing the top back part if my head with one hand, and the back of my neck with his other pulling me closer to his lower person, I display no resistance as it went deeper into my throat, I gag a little but open more to receive his long woody. He's pleased. I stick my tongue out as far as it can go and tickle his balls as he fucks my throat sliding in and out of it. Gently I squeeze my clit's pearl then slip two fingers into my hot wet pussy.

Carefully stroking the upper most part lining. He pulls himself out of my mouth and motions for me to get on my knees, I oblige and he pulls my hair and grabs under my jaw and pushes himself back in. With both hands he drives my head back and forth onto his nice size cock, going faster and faster. As he released his load I explode and came in the bath. His load hit the back of my throat with a fierce power I felt like I was drowning, starting to cough and choke,

I catch myself, opening my eyes dropping my legs back down into the water I scoot myself back up to a normal sitting position. I look around to see, that I was still alone. Feeling good from the pleasure I have given myself, I lean back and take my breasts into my hands rubbing them as I wonder to myself, "is that what it would be like with "HIM".

Chapter 3

Greg

I looked down at her apartment but I didn't care about the eyes that could be watching me. I was craving that woman and I didn't care if the world knew I was sitting out here with my swollen man in my hand. To be honest I like being watched. It only turns me on more. My eyes travel back to her apartment window and that's when I see her walking back into the room. She had a small red towel wrapped around her. She looked amazing and even sexier than before. She had been in bathroom for a while so I couldn't help but wonder who was watching me. I guess I'm not the only one living around here that likes to watch.

When I started to focus on her that's when she dropped her towel. I know she still knew I was sitting out here. With the rain falling heavy and lighting still lighting up the sky, and all the while my man still jumping because he hasn't find his release yet. I couldn't get that until she came back. There's nothing like exploding when you watching and thinking about fucking a sexy woman. My manhood is extra wet now from the rain. Watching her stand there, body wet from her bath made me start to pre'cum. I want to be deep inside of her right now. She just doesn't know how close I am to knocking on her door so I can give her what we both been wanting.

My man pulsed as that thought came across my mind and it only makes me move my hand faster. Lighting lights the sky once more and that's when we made eye contact. I watch as she drops her towel and cuffs her breasts. My mouth opens and my hand stops mid stoke; her eyes never leave mine. When she turns around I see that her ass is big and round, and all I could think about was hitting that big ass from the back. It isn't long before she sits down on her bed and pushes back a little. I start moving my hand again the rain covers me once more. I watch as she opens her legs and not once does she stop looking at me. I don't know how long I've been waiting for this scene to play out but I'm glad it's happening tonight.

I move my hand faster and I can feel the pleasure moving through my body, but I can't lose focus because I don't want to miss a thing. Now she is touching her secret place and spreading it open. I damn near blast one right then. I want to jump up and run to her. She starts rubbing her clit and it wasn't a fast movement so I followed her pace as I moved my hand up and down my dick. The faster she moves her fingers the faster my movements go. Her head falls back and I can see her mouth opening and I know she is making noise. What I wouldn't give to hear the pleasure sounds coming from her lips.

My dick hardens even more and I know I am close to the edge. I can't take my eyes off of her, as my nut flies up in the air like a soda that had been shaken before you open it. I could tell then that she exploded too as she lays back on the bed breathing heavy. I close my eyes taking in the mental picture before I get up and walk inside my condo a very satisfied man.

Susan

Entering my bedroom feeling relaxed and comfortable, I sashay in, wiggling everything that shakes. I let the towel drop, reached up to my breasts and giving them a firm squeeze, subconsciously knowing I am being watched. I wondered quite a few things about my observer, but one thing I knew for sure... He has to be single. Any man on the balcony in the rain for an extensive amount of time has to be, a psycho, a perv, or just plain ol' crazy! Either way I became very curious... Mental note; "*When I get to the office tomorrow, I'll have The Law Firm's investigator do me a huge favor and look into this guys background*". I'd hate to be in the next drama/suspense movie on Lifetime.

I reached for my "Love Spell" by Victoria Secret, sat on my bed's edge closest toward the window, and slowly work the lotion on my body from the feet up. Holding each leg up in the air I work my hands down enticingly seductive that has got to be a turn on... as if I don't have his attention already. I can't get the ass covered siting on it, so I stand with ease, turn around and facing my mirror, rub one hand over one cheek at a time. Then I turn again as if I need to see that healthy ass in the mirror.

Slowly, patiently, massaging my inner

thighs, reaching the gap in between Ahhh, very tempted to just stop doing what I'm doing and work hand magic on my luscious almost wet pussy. I pause then go up my stomach around my waist and sides, stopping at my breasts which are very perky, nipples erect. I know... feel him watching. I hope he's enjoying the show.

I climb up into my bed slowly, like a panther stalking her prey. I stop short and roll over to my back. The flashes of lightening almost make this act look sinister. I place a hand at my forehead rubbing my hair backwards and the other hand on my thigh. I slide it up to the point where I can feel my wetness wanting so desperately to escape me. I place my middle finger at the top center of my kat just teasing it.

My back arches up off the bed with my knees up, feet planted firmly. I continue to rub until my legs open wider, placing two fingers inside then back out up to my mouth. Slowly I lick both fingers together, and slide them in tasting myself becoming more aroused. I go back down to my lower section and continue to please myself, now with both hands, one back to my wet pussy and the other to my ass from behind.

I love getting myself off with two fingers in and my thumb pleasing my clit, I wiggle a finger into my ass and patiently slide it in and out. Before long I release my cream, all over my hand, down my ass, and leaving a juicy wet spot beneath me. Overly exhausted I slip into the land of dreams with my last thoughts on... I'll change the sheets tomorrow.

Chapter 4

Greg

I turned around once more and looked back at the most beautiful woman, laying there motionless. So many emotions are passing through me that I don't even know where to begin. It is like we shared a moment or a night of endless love making without actually touching one other. I made my way to the bathroom so I could get out of these wet cloths and into a hot shower.

I looked at myself in my full length mirror and wondered why I am alone. I'm not a bad looking man. I'm tall and with a nice body, tight abs, you could see the strength that my body progress. I turned on the shower sticking my hand inside testing the water before stepping in. The water isn't too hot just cool enough to quench the fire that is still burning inside. I put my head under the water and let it run down my heated face. The water feels like little fingers working magic on my tense muscles.

I don't know how long I was under the water but it was past cold when I stepped out. I couldn't help wondering why a beautiful lady like that would play sex games with a total stranger. The storm is still going full force as I slide under the cool covers. My desire is satisfied for tonight, but my body is still calling out to the stranger in the condos across from me.

Even in sleep I'm not free of the fire that burned inside from that hot and sexy neighbor of mine.

She invades my dreams. Dreams that are so real I can swear I am touching her, tasting her, and kissing her. I can hear the sounds she was making so clearly. I want to wake up, but I can't either. My arm reaches out and touches the cold empty spot beside me letting me know it was just a dream.

I look at over at my clock and see it is nearly four am and the sound of the rain is still going full force. I laid there looking out my window wandering is she up and can't sleep too. I am so tempted to get up and see if she was still laying in the same spot she was in when I came inside. I roll over and moan as I punch my pillow. I refuse to get out of bed and turn myself into a damn stalker. I stare off in space and come to the conclusion that I am going to make it my business to meet this sexy lady as soon as possible.

Susan

My alarm clock goes off, "Wow, 7am already" I thought to myself. No time to lay here for another hour, I have a few matters I need to square away before I punch that clock. I immediately get up and snatch the sheets off with me. Walking toward the hamper, I glance out my window up to the one-night-stand balcony and don't see anything resembling the figure of the night. I know this was more than a horny imagination... The phone rings... caller ID reading Fort Bragg's wonder why Tom would be calling me from the base and not overseas?

"Hello?"

"Hello Miss Hatchet please".

"This is she."

The voice on the other end paused. "This is Commander Pennywell speaking; I am calling this morning in regards of Corporal Tom G. O'Dell".

"In regards of... Is everything ok with Tom?"

"Well Ma'am, no not at all. He left two emergency contact numbers, in which case we called both at his request. So I called to let you know that there was a tragic accident at Tom's station and well... Well Tom didn't make it Ma'am".

"Oh my God; what happened?"

"Sorry Ma'am I'm not at liberty to discuss details, someone will be contacting you soon with arrangement details. Sorry for your loss and I do apologize for contacting you this way with this news. Good-day Ma'am." And the phone went dead.

I thought about Tom's wife and poor kids... Damn! I put the phone down and went to the shower. In and out, then I got dressed feeling like a house just fell on me. I still have to go in today. I hurry to my car backed out the garage and drove on to work.

Making a pit stop at Starbucks for my daily ritual, I really didn't feel much like breakfast but I still ordered my usual. I known Tom for 10 years now; I was a freshman and he a senior... Damn Tom why! Making my way into the office, I put on my beautiful day at the office face and rushed to Dan's office, glad that he was in.

"Hey Dan."

"Hello Susan." he replied. "How are you this morning?"

"I'm good Dan how's the wife and kids?"

"They're all ok." he says; with a puzzled look on his face.

I looked into his eyes; "Tom was killed in Iraq last-night while I was making out with my neighbor."

"Oh Susan you naughty girl."

I interrupted, "Not like that, anyway long story. Here run this address and find out who is leasing or owns this Condo. Then run the name and leave the file on my desk."

No questions, Dan just replied; "I'm on it Suzy Q". A nickname he and some other collage Frat' Brothers called me from the Hostess cakes I was so well known for always having.

I turned heading for my office. "Thanks Dan." I shouted from down the hall. I stopped at my secretary's desk to retrieve my messages and walked into my office.

As I sat at my desk thinking back to last-night I was feeling bothered, but not in the way of receiving terrible news, but more like curiously horny.

I started day-dreaming, imagining "HIM" right there in my office, door closed trousers down around his ankles. He scoots over to where I am sitting, grabs my hair from the back of my head and pushes his long hard dick into my mouth. I take it... Mmmmmmm. I suck, caressing his balls and he moans.

Then he reaches down lifting me out the chair, and bending me over my desk. I'm in love. He enters my dripping wet pussy and pushes himself in deep. I groan sort of loud and he puts his hand over my mouth and stroking me like he is pounding a late night hooker in the ally. "Ohhh ohhh I'm cumming, I'm cum"... A knock on the door⋯ I snap out of it and regain my composure.

"Yes come in."

Chapter 5

Greg

Sleep never came that night. So as soon as day break arrived I got up made myself some coffee and headed out for my morning jog. I run from 5 to 10 miles every morning no matter how the weather. Most people think I'm crazy but I'm just a health fanatic. I didn't get this body by laying around eating donuts all day. That's the problem with so many cops today. Once they've been police for a few years, they just let themselves go, oh no not me, but that wasn't my problem today.

My problem was that spit fire of a lady in apartment 3J, and just as she crossed my mind she pulled to a stop at the red light on the corner of Stevens and Central. We made eye contact for a moment, but I could tell that she didn't know that she was looking at her late night lover. As soon as she rode pass I looked at her tag number. I might as well find out as much information as I can about her, because it doesn't look like I'm going to be able to break this obsession with her. I gave her a nod and continued on down the street.

As I ran flashes of our night was breaking my concentration and my jog was getting too dangerous for my health. I had to admit it to myself she was becoming an addiction and if I don't have her soon, I didn't know what I would do.

So I cut my run short and headed back to the house. It wasn't long before I was out of the shower and driving to the precinct.

"Good morning Sgt. Brown."

I looked over at the young rookie and said, " Good morning son do I have any messages?"

"No sir you don't."

"Thanks. Is Captain Williams in his office?"

"Yes, Sgt."

"Good, if I get any calls pass them into his office." I said as I walked away.

In the background all I heard were phones ringing as I knocked on the door and walked inside. The last thing I heard before I closed the door behind me was, "Homicide" My best friend since elementary looked up from a file he was reading

"What's up Greg? This isn't like you to be here so early."

"Now what makes you thinks something's up?"

"Boy I been knowing you for over 30 years and as soon as you walked into my office I knew something was wrong so you might as well have a seat and s

Susan

"Good morning Susan," said Mr. Kanaski.

"Good morning Boss, how was your evening?"

"It was spectacular. The Mrs.'s and I had a great time, and I just wanted to drop by and say thank you for the tickets."

"No problem Sir, enjoy your day." He was walking out my office displaying a smile of a lucky man. "Excuse me Sir. Have you seen John this morning?"

"He was investigating one of our high profile cases and I was sure he'd have something for me this morning. But no I haven't seen or heard from him yet.

"Well it's still early."

"By the way, my deepest condolences for your loss, try not to work too hard today." He walks off as I sit there looking puzzled.

I never mentioned Tom to anyone who wasn't in my immediate circle of *"need to know personal business"*, but that's the one thing about H.K I never knew how or who he got his Intel from, but he had always been proficient.

Harvey Kanaski, fresh out of Harvard with enough money to buy someone like Stevie Jobs over 5 times. He inherited this law firm from his daddy who died of an aneurism over 40 years ago.

He took me on when I was just an intern at Yale. He saw something in me that I didn't see in myself... I still didn't, but I suspected it must be my ambition or my drive.

I had a thing for law since the days of the Jeffery Dormer case. My late Uncle was one of his victims and was completely crushed my mother. The depression got her addicted to psych meds and she's never been the same. My phone rings...

"Hello, Susan speaking."

"Hey Susan, its Anthony. John was murdered this morning. Right now all I know is that he was sitting at a red light sipping a cup of coffee two masked men pulled up alongside of him and left part of his skull and brains scattered on the driver's side window."

"Oh my God." One thing about Anthony, he never sugar coats nothing for me. "Was there anything he was working on that might be of interest to me?"

"Well, the case of the murdered wife is all I know of, but are you going over there?"

"Yes, I got a call from Captain Williams requiring my presence on this one due to unusual circumstances; police and forensics are already there."

"Ok, I'm on my way too. Don't let them take anything as evidence until I get there, he may have had some information for me, which has something to do with his demise. I will fill you in when I get there, I'm on my way."

"See you soon Sue."

I hang up, rub my hair back, put my hands on my face and take a breather. Anthony is the leading CSI for the FBI. We go back since the good old college days. My circle of friends are 90% of people in law enforcement which at times. means, we cross paths working cases together. I grabbed my purse heading out my office, I instruct my secretary to forward all my calls to my cell, I see it's going to be a long day.

Chapter 6

Greg

Charles sat there looking from the file he was holding up to me waiting for an answer to his question.

"Are you going to answer me or we just going to sit here looking at each other all morning. "

"You wouldn't believe it if I told you."

"Try me." Charles said as he laid the file down on his crowded desk.

I wanted to tell him but somehow I was just too embarrassed. But I decided to just let it all out. I told him how I'd been watching my neighbor for weeks, and I didn't stop until I told him about the scene we played out last night. When I was finally finished he sat behind his desk looking at me with big wide eyes.

"Well what do you have to say?" I asked him. He almost had me sitting on the edge of my chair waiting for his response.

"Damn!" Was the only words that came out of Charles mouth.

"Damn that's it. You telling me your best friend have been making a fool out of him self and all you can say is damn?"

As soon as Charles was about to speak his phone started to ring; "Wait a second." Charles says as he raises a finger up in the air. "Captain Williams here."

I sat back listening to part of his phone call after seeing that we weren't going to be able to finish this conversation right now I got up to head to my office, but the sound of Charles voice stopped me.

"Hey don't go too far we have a homicide." Charles said with his hand placed over the receiver.

"Yeah I kind of figured that. I'll be in my office when you're ready."

I closed the door behind me and made my way to the break room I needed another cup of coffee, and then I'm going to find out who this spit fire of a lady is across from me. I poured myself a cup of strong coffee and closed the door to my office. I typed in her tag number and her picture popped right up. There she was big as day and Susan was her name. Well it looks like you are about to meet your match I said to her photo.

She's some big time lawyer I see. I smiled because that's a good thing that we are in the same profession. I sat there staring at her picture on my screen and reading through her back ground until Charles opened my door.

"Okay lets bounce we have some big shot lawyers waiting for us at the crime scene."

I grabbed my suit jacket off the back of my chair and slid my gun into my holster closing the office door behind me, Man this day is already starting off bad. A murder first thing in the morning. I haven't even had my breakfast yet. These my last thoughts as I followed Charles out the precinct.

Susan

As I entered the parking garage, I hit the car alarm as I would usually do. After the short "whoop whoop" of the alarm, there was a large force of hot wind pushing me back into the elevator and into the back wall. Down I went. As I slid down the wall, I look up and see a large inferno headed toward me as the doors close in the nick−of−time.

"What the fuck?" I quickly jump to my feet pushing the level 2 button. I've got to get to my car.

There were more explosions as the elevator shook briefly before reaching level two. The doors open and I peeked out looking around as I reach in my purse for my keys. I hit the alarm and got the short audible tone once again... No explosions. I quickly rush to my car and jump in. Starting the car I reach for my cell and place it on the car charger.

"Call H.K." the phone speed dials.

"Hello"

"Hey Harvey. There was an explosion in the parking garage on level one."

"Yes Sue, I am quite aware. We are currently evacuating the building now. Apparently one of the company cars was equipped to..."

"Well who could that have been meant for? No one utilizes the same car daily unless out on the road for several days."

"I don't know any more than you do Sue, are you ok."

"Yes I was still in the elevator, but I went for my own car and actually out of the building now."

"Look Sweetie I got to go, I have a lot going on here and the FBI seems to be here already... They are never usually this quick. I smell a rat" .Harvey hung up as I reached the intersection where John was murdered.

I park and sit for a second to gather my thoughts and calm myself. Looking in the rearview I see debris in my hair and Anthony approaching behind me. I open the door and step out.

"Good morning Tony,"

"Hey Susie, come with me". I shut the door and briskly follow closely behind him.

Tony used to work out heavily playing sports most his life, but mostly he was a sprint runner in College. We approach the caution tape and Anthony shows his credentials and motions to the officers on duty. "She's with me".

They let us through. I see a body in the front seat uncovered. Forensics was taking pictures and dusting for prints. I see two files and a manila envelope with my name on it, sitting there on the front passenger seat. I go to reach for the items and Tony stops me cold.

"Susie, that's evidence. I will get it to you as soon as the locals get done doing what they need to do."

Just then an unmarked car pulls up and two officers get out; neither one in uniform, so they must be higher up the chain of command. They walk over to Anthony and shake hands. Anthony introduces me to Capt. Williams, and Capt. Williams introduces Sgt. Brown to Anthony and me. We all greet each other, but the eye contact of Sgt. Brown seems awkwardly familiar.

Chapter 7

Greg

As soon as the car pulled to a stop I noticed my neighbor's car right off. I looked around the scene before my hand touched the door handle.

"Are you coming Brown are not?"

"Yeah I'm coming."

"What's the hell wrong with you? You had been acting funny all morning."

"It's nothing really let's go." I opened the door and went right to work by looking over the scene. Once the lawyers were introduced to us I knew for a fact that it was my little spit fire. Damn she's even sexier up close. Our eyes meet and I could tell that she felt like she knew me. I didn't look away. I just held my eye contact until she tried to shake my hand.

When she touched me it ignited the fire inside of me. I had to have her. It took me a moment to drop her hand but it didn't take me long to realize we were getting looks from my partner and her companion. I cleared my throat and tune all my attention on the scene in front of us. I continued to watch her as she shot off question after question and I knew then that she was good at what she do.

I walked off. I couldn't take being around her any longer. I wanted to speak to her, try to get to know her but this wasn't the time or the place. I started walking around the car that the body was in. I could see that he had been shot at least twice in the head, and the back door of the vehicle was slightly open letting me know that someone had to have been hiding in the back of his car. The poor man never had a chance.

When I walked around to the passenger side of the car that's when I saw some files that had Susie's name on it. I put on a pair of gloves and reached inside to pick them up.

"What do you think you're doing?" Susie asked from behind me.

"I'm begging up evidence what does it look."

"Look Sgt. Brown I really need those files." Susan said as her eyes went from me to the folders.

"And Susan, may I call you that?"

"Yes, but you don't understand."

"Oh I understand completely why you need them." I looked over at Williams and he was still speaking with the officers that were on the scene. "If I could help you Susan I would, but this has to be cleared before anything gets turned over to you."

She looked down for a second and I could see how important this was to her but if this guy got killed for what was inside one of these folders then she could be in danger too, and I can't let anything happen to her if I could help it. She looked at me with those big brown eyes. Damn I knew they were brown and I could tell that she knew what I was thinking, but she didn't say anything.

"Come on Susan let's go." I put my hand in the middle of her back and she stopped for a moment and looked at me.

"I wandered what it would feel like for you to touch me. I just didn't think I find out this way." She said and then she walked off, leaving me standing there with my mouth wide open.

Susan

I was feeling awkward around Sgt. Brown; it was almost like we were supposed to meet. I watched as he placed on the latex gloves ready to go to work. His frame was tall next to mine; I must admit I felt slightly enticed by his stature. I could tell by his height and build he was holding a package that I needed to explore. Just then I snapped back to reality as Sgt. Brown picked up what was for me in the front seat.

I walked over to him I had to ask for those files. Even if he wouldn't give them to me I was hoping he would allow me a look-see. I felt stunned being told NO! He wasn't rude, just stern with a firm tone, but more caring, as it seemed like he was appointed to be my guardian angel.

Then he touched me... How dare he do that! But I felt warm, it felt magnetic. I put on my grown woman *"walk away tantrum"* as if I didn't hear or understand a word he said, but I turned briefly and got me another glimpse of the hunk of a man standing there in a beater and boxers with a look on his face like you know you want me. Well that was my minds thoughts on it, and if I was right Mr. Brown... I sure do.

Meanwhile... Catching up with Anthony and Capt. Williams, "Excuse me gentlemen Anthony can I have a word with you please."

It didn't take long for Anthony to join me once he pulled himself away from the Captain.

"Anthony I need to see those files. If there is anything there that John discovered in his investigation that is the cause of his death, I would know."

"That's why we are here Sue. They're just about done anyway. I will be able to talk to the Captain soon. This doesn't appear to be an FBI case so I'm out of my jurisdiction, but I was called here for my expertise."

We walked back over to the Captain as he was just ordering the scene cleaned up, and just in time too, as an Eyewitness News van pulled up. I can tell you I do not need any more press, not right now. Anthony was still talking to Brown as my phone rang. It was Rick briefing me on the Intel he gathered for me, I hung up the phone not shocked at all.

"Susan, Susan," Tony called out. "Where are you going?"

"Press Tony, I don't need that right now, call me when you can."

I got in the car and pulled off, but first I made a called to my boss; I had to find out if it was safe to go back to the office or if we were meeting at one of the local branches. It only took a second to brief him on the scene and I let him know I wasn't able to get the file or a little peek-a-boo.

"Oh before I forget to tell you. Even through the building's safe don't use the parking garage."

"Oh that's just great. Parking is horrific and I have to walk from God knows where in these heels."

He chuckled.

"Hold on my other line is ringing."

I switch lines... It was Tony saying that he arranged for me to see the contents of what was in the manila envelope with my name on it, but I had to meet one of the officers from the scene. So I agreed.

When I switched back over, Harvey was gone. I figured as much. Can't keep a busy man on hold, especially when he's the boss. I sent him a quick text: *Harvey I'm making a quick stop before I come back in. I have a lunch date with Sgt. Brown.*

Chapter 8

Greg

I watched as Susan got inside of her car and drove away. I knew she was upset somehow I could feel it inside of me. I don't understand how I could feel so connected to someone I only just physically met. Yes, we played as strangers maybe to me that's where our bond was made. Two lonely people who needed someone special in their lives. I kept asking myself, *"How come I'm just noticing her lately? It's no telling how long she lived across from me. Why now?"* I closed my eyes and I can see how firm her ass looked as she walked away. How much I want to see that ass bended down in front of me. She is sexy as hell. Nice breasts just the kind of woman I'm looking for

. "Brown can I speak to you for a second please?" The FBI officer asked as he walked over to me.

What the hell does he want with me? I don't even understand why he's even here.

"Yes how may I help you?"

"There will be a female lawyer returning here. You know the one that was here earlier? She will arrive soon to look through those files that were inside the victim's car to make sure nothing important concerning the cases he was working on was inside."

"I will do my best to help the lady out as much as possible, but nothing can be given to her until it is cleared by the Captain."

"Yes sir, I understand completely. Just make sure you inform Susan of that. Thanks for your time Brown."

So Susan would be returning here, but I had something else better in mind. Our next meeting wouldn't be us standing over a dead body either.

"Charles let's go if that lawyer wants to see me let her come to the office." I said and headed for the car.

As we started to pull off I let down my window and told the only officer left on the scene to tell the female lawyer where she could locate me at when she returned.

"Damn Greg there you go again on this crazy shit." Charles said not even taking his eyes off the road. "Do you know that lady?"

"No why you ask me that?" Dammit I knew our eye contact was noticeable.

"Greg how long have we been cops?"

"Long enough."

"You're right long enough to know when I see you acting suspicious."

"Suspicious what are you talking about?" I tried to laugh it off.

"Go ahead and laugh all you want Greg, but I know you're up to something, and it has something to do with that damn lawyer chick."

Susan

I wasn't sure, but back at the crime scene I remembered that there was a 2012 all black Escalade with tinted windows just sitting there. It seemed unoccupied from afar and I was able to make out the tags. Looking in my rearview I could see the same tag, New York plates. I didn't make any sudden moves to alert suspicion, just kept going about my way like I do every day.

I was kind of upset that Sgt. Brown had changed where we were going to meet but now I am glad that he did because I wouldn't have noticed them before.

Arriving at my destination, I parked and reached in the glove box to retrieve my fire arm. A prosecutor with a gun, not common by any standards, but I thank good ol' Daddy for insisting I join the Army ROTC and go to the reserves. Now this down home backwoods Georgia girl can handle her own.

Now that I had a moment to myself I was sitting here, thinking, while my engine still running... *"Was that car rigged bomb intended for me? Why was this SUV tailing me?"*

I placed a quick call... "6th Squad 4th district, Officer Riley speaking, how may I help you?"

"Yes this is Susan; may I speak to a Sgt.

Brown?"

"I'm sorry Ma'am Sgt. Brown isn't with the 6th, would you like me to transfer you?"

"Yes by all means, it's urgent."

While I was placed on hold I could see the SUV still parked half a block away. I turn on the radio, inserted a CD *(Today We Have Us by Atlantamoody)* and selected track 4. A Diva by right and a songstress by trade, she was and still is the hottest act Motown hasever come out with. Second on the charts under Michael Jackson of course, whose career makes him "King" of the pop era.

Sitting in my car outside of Hibachi's, I look up in the rearview and it's still there, watching me like prey to a vulture in the desert heat. "Knock knock knock" I jumped by the sound. Luckily it was only Sgt. Brown tapping on my window.

"Ready to go in?" he asked.

"Yes, excuse me for one second." I said reaching for my side arm and placeing it back in the glove box before stepping out of the car.

Brown asks jokingly, "Got a permit for that thing?

"Sure do." I replied, quickly adding "Are you always a cop?"

Now both of us were smiling like two teenagers with crushes, he responds, "Only when

I'm protecting the very beautiful public from the worst society has to offer."

"I guess that sort of makes us colleagues, you lock them up, and I put them away." We laugh, making our way toward the entrance of the restaurant.

"Come here often."

"No, I rarely have time to make it out of the office for lunch,"

"Ladies first." with a hand gesture like an usher in the movie theatre escorting patrons to their seats. First thing comes to mind is that old saying, *"An officer and a gentleman."*

Chapter 9

Greg

I stood aside and waited for her to walk in the restaurant. My eyes traced her body from her head all the way down to her nice size butt and thick thighs. I love watching this woman walk. There wasn't anything sexier to me than an educated woman carrying a gun. What she just did only made me want her more.

As we were seated I took a minute and looked around making sure that she was as much protected as she could be out in the open. Something was going on and it looked like she just got right in the middle of it.

"What are you looking around like that for?" Susan asked and looking around too.

"Oh it's nothing just checking the place out. Never really been here before."

I looked up as the waiter stopped at our table. We placed our orders and I decided that it was time for us to get down to business.

"Here," I said laying the folder down on the table. "Just remember Susan you can only look and see if there's anything you need inside of these files."

"What if I need something that's inside?"

"Then you have to wait until I get it cleared.

"Cleared? How long would that take?" She asked as she opened up the file.

I watched her as she scanned the papers. I could tell that she knew what she was looking for. Why do I have a feeling she had been playing me this whole time.

"So do you need anything?" She looked up at me with a small smile on her face. Sgt. Brown asks.

"As a matter of fact yes I do need something."

"You do and what is that?" I asked her while I started to pull the file out of her hands.

"Sgt. I need this whole file because this right here just made this whole case a hell of a lot easier."

Is this lady serious? How in the hell was I supposed to give her our whole evidence folder. There was no way in hell I could pull that off even if I did decide to help her.

"Susan I can't do that I'm sorry."

"So there's no way you can help me at all?"

It was a way I could help her but something was telling me to hold back. She already had someone following her. Hell I saw that much myself. If I give her this information all I would be doing is putting her in danger. She turned those big brown eyes on me and it nearly melted my heart.

"Please this will help me a lot Brown."

As soon as I felt my guard slipping the waiting arrived with our food. Thank God he had perfect timing.

Susan

I couldn't believe what I was seeing. As I viewed the content of the files, I saw that the evidence John had discovered got him killed, and it cracked our case wide open. Since Mr. Barlow hasn't taken the plea that was offered to him, I can take that off the table and move forward with the death penalty. I could see now that Brown doesn't seem willing to make this easier.

The waiter arrives with our food as I closed the folder. As he was leaving I opened the Manila envelope with my name on it.

I knocked over my drink. "What the fuck?"

Brown looked over at me and I could hear him ask me if I was okay, but I couldn't get a word out. When I looked back down he saw what my eyes were glued on. A stack of freshly printed $100 dollar bills a letter addressed to the law firm in regards to me and a key that said *"Wells Fargo"* on it. I looked up at Brown, feeling the warmth emulating from his eyes. I knew at that moment that was a man that I can trust.

"No I'm not alright. I think we need to leave here right away and go somewhere safe. Brown this letter has several names on it implicating key people in law enforcement, both local PD and FBI, along with two judges."

Brown stood up from his seat, "Come on

Sue, and let's get you out of here. I know of a place you can go."

I stood up while Brown dropped a hundred on the table for the lunch we never ate,

"I thought you were hungry?"

He leaned over picked up his knife and fork sliced through his mouth watering steak and placed a bite size piece in his mouth. I watched thinking to myself... those lips, sexy, juicy, teasing me, and up comes the fork to my mouth.

"Here Sue have some."

I opened my mouth as he watched me take the piece of meat from his fork. I had meat partially hanging out; he takes a finger and gently makes sure I get it all. We walk toward the door as two black suited men enter looking around.

Brown eyed both men wearing dark shades as well as I did. They didn't make a scene just stepped aside and let us walk out. I headed right for my car, but Brown stopped me.

"No Sue, my car." I looked at him with questioning eyes. "I'm quite sure they ran your plates and will know exactly who you are before we get back to your place."

He grabbed my hand and leaded me to his car. Such passion I feel in the smooth skin of a man in this line of work, but I can tell he keeps himself up; we'll groomed, tight physique, and fresh breath. I took notice of when we were chest to chest passing through the two men at the door.

We get to Browns car and without missing a beat, he opened the door on the passenger side and says, "Ladies first."

I get in and sit down as he closes the door behind me. As he walked around to the driver's side, I watch never taking my eyes off of him. When he got in all I could do is blurt out

Chapter 10

Greg

Man was I surprised. No I was more than surprised; as a no matter of fact surprised is not a good enough word for what I'm feeling right now. I looked over at Sue. She had the folder pushed up against her chest with a look of shock still showing on her face.

"Are you ok Sue?" I asked her.

"Yes, I am." She paused for a moment. "Did you see all that money?"

"Oh yeah I saw it and you do know now that you can't be left alone anymore. You are in way over your head and if we are dealing with law enforcements agents that far up the ladder then there's no telling who had your friend killed. I didn't know he was the lawyer in the high profile case that's been in the news for the past few months."

"Brown I have to have this folder."

"Sue we been through this before, plus you have more important things to worry about then that damn folder."

I started the car and started too pulled away; that's when I noticed the two men exiting the restaurant. This wasn't good at all.

"Where are we going?"

"We're going somewhere safe for now." I turned my lights and sirens on and headed up Riverside back toward the precinct.

I was looking in my rear view mirror the whole way there and sure enough they were right behind us. I don't know why I felt so protective of Susan, but I do and I can't let anything happen to her. I damn sure can't let anyone get their hands on that file. That folder could bring down a lot of important people.

It didn't take me long to reach the station and I decided it was best not to rely on anyone right now. Hell for all I know there could be a mole in this station too. If a cover up is going on it would make since to commit the murder around a precinct where they had someone inside so they could keep them informed on all information.

I parked the police car and got out and walked around to the passenger side. I opened the door for Susan, and for the first time I was glad that this precinct had an underground parking lot that only allowed police inside. I know for a fact they weren't one of our men but they were cops or FBI.

Sue walked over to the elevator and pushed the button.

"Sue we not going inside, come on." I said as I took her still shaking hand and headed in the direction of the employees parking. I hit the alarm on my dark grey Chrysler 300 as soon as we rounded the corner.

"I need to get a few things from my place." Sue said as we turned out of the parking lot.

"You can't go back there. Believe me when I say they are watching your place because they know sooner or later you are going to turn back up there."

"So are we going to yours?" She asked as she turned those big brown eyes on me.

"No we're not going anywhere near there."

"Oh," was the last thing she said as she turned and looked out of the passenger side window.

Susan

As we road I continued to try to figure out what was going on. I had so much on my mind that I got to the point that I really didn't care where we were going as long as I was safe. We approached a small beach house about two hours outside of town,

"Brown where are we?" I asked as he pushed a button on a small white box clipped to his sun visor.

"It's a place my father owns. He used to come here a lot until he retired from the force".

The garage door opened and we pulled in. Once we got inside I saw that it was a cozy little place but it looked as no one has been here for years.

"I don't get down here much. Work has been so tremendously demanding that I hadn't taken a vacation in over two years. My niece comes by every 3 months or so to keep this old place up." He reached out and tapped me on my arm. "Hey Sue, here's my cell," as he searches though his contact list for a number. "Type in everything you may need from your place to last for a month, and I will have someone pick them up".

"Ok." I agreed, but wondered how they will get into my apartment, but hell, I didn't ask.

Brown picks up the house phone, dials a

number, and then says to the party on the other end, "This is Gregory, I'd like the usual and make that two please," there's a pause before he speaks again, "Yes, thank you" then he hangs up.

Lunch had passed so I take it he had ordered a little something for dinner. We did skip lunch. He gave me a quick tour of the place.

"Get comfortable and make yourself at home. We are going to be here for a while."

It wasn't long before I typed in a list of clothing, accessories, along with some female hygiene products and my laptop, then hit send. After placing the cellphone on the coffee table, I went into one the back rooms which had its own private bathroom. I came back out in my sports bra. It looked nice with a pair of shorts that I saw folded on a shelf in the bathroom. A little big on me, but with a drawstring, I conveniently tied to help keep them up. I looked up at Brown, standing only two feet away.

"Them shorts look good on you."

Tears started streaming my cheeks, dripping off my chin, and landing on my breasts.

Brown rushed over to me. "Are you ok Sue?"

I stood there looking up at this charming man in a suit, as he wrapped his rather strong arms around me ever so gently, caressing me with such a warming passion, and rubbing my back as if I was his long lost wife, but I felt as though this embrace was much more than that.

This was the heat of ones passion that were never ending for a new love. I rested my head on his chest and placed my arms around his waist. As I tried to finish what I was going to say, he said, "Shhh not another word, I know... I know exactly what you're feeling right now.

I was always easy to read by the opposite sex.

Chapter 11

Greg

She looked at me with those brown eyes and they just pulled me in. How could this little lady have a strong hold on me like that? The tears in her eyes continued to fall and I couldn't help myself. I took a finger and traced the path of her tears. I wiped away tear after tear without even taking my eyes off of her.

She felt so good in my arms and all I wanted to do was pull her closer. I lowered my head until our lips touched. I was hoping she would pull away but she did the opposite and moved into my kiss. I felt the fire as soon as her lips touched mine. I was lost. My mind, body, and soul all belonged to her with just one simple kiss.

I had this little voice in my head yelling at me to stop just pull away but as soon as I started to, she put her arms around my neck and pulled me back down. Damn why she had to do that? It was a lost cause then. I deepen the kiss as my hands moved up and down her half naked back. Her skin was so warm and soft just like I imagine it would be.

I broke the kiss only for a second as I

started to trace my lips down the side of her neck. I didn't stop until I reached her shoulder. She moved her head to the side and moaned. Damn she sounded so sexy.

I lifted my head up and broke the kiss once again. I know I was wrong for taking advantage of the situation,

"Sue we need to stop." I said as I started to kiss her shoulder once again.

"But what if I don't want you to?"

"Then you sexy lady would be in trouble because I am so wanting to be inside of you right now."

"Then what's stopping you because I sure am not?"

When she looked at me I knew she meant business. She wanted me just as much as I wanted her. I lifted her up and she wrapped her legs around my hips. I didn't waste any more time finding her mouth. I dropped down on my knees and laid her down on the sofa and trace the curves of her breasts with my tongue. I wanted her and I wanted her now. I took her month again but this time with force. She moaned against my lips just loving the feeling that it was bringing her, until there was a knock on the door.

Susan

I tried to fight back my tears, but what I felt for Tom just wouldn't let me. It just hit me all at once that I may not even be able to attend his service with what's going on now. Then there was John. He hadn't been at The Law Firm all that long, but we had developed a strong bond as co-workers. I always did admire his sweet little wife Helen.

This was my case and he was doing me a favor that got him killed. Knowing that I had to let Tom go, everything about Brown seemed so right. As he embraced me, giving me a kiss I knew this had to be for me. It didn't make sense, but it didn't need to. I was open and straight forward; Brown seemed to want it too, but at times pulling away. I knew his heart as if he was someone I'd known all my life.

He wasn't intimidated; he was honest, and respectful. Great qualities, I respect and accept, but right now I wanted him. I gave a little push as he leaned in for the next kiss, and ran my hand across the small of his back, around his waist, down his side, around to the his front, and over his already stiff dick.

It was long, thick, erect, and pushing forward, wanting so bad to be freed from beyond that zipper. I grab it, and then quickly try to release it, continuing with a light rub down the poll then back up to the belt buckle. As I was undoing the belt, there's a knock at the door.

I jump, startled by being taken out of my heat zone, and nervous as to whom this could be? Brown felt me tense up, grabbing his dick once again, but a little tighter due to the interruption that came calling at the front door. He placed a hand on my shoulder and his other hand on mine holding on to his baby maker.

"It's ok Baby", he said as he used his hands to guide me away from him. "No one could find us here. This place is safe and totally untraceable." Relax while I get that, it's probably just the food".

I released him even though I really didn't want to. I could have held on to him forever. I walk over to the dining area and take a seat. All pouty eyed, lips poked out.

"Ok you get the food and hurry back so I can get my dessert." He looked back at me with a smile.

Chapter 12

Greg

I pulled my shirt down over my harden man. I didn't need to be showing all my business to no damn delivery man, but I couldn't help but smiled at the words that came out of her sexy mouth. I know she's not talking about no dessert when I been waiting to feast of her since the first time I saw her walk across her bedroom window.

My mind drifted back to the first night I saw her. I was sitting out on my balcony just star gazing because I wasn't into looking in women windows then. Well not women just hers. I don't know what made me look her way that night, but I was sure damn glad that I did. She stood there right in front of the window and dropped her towel. I nearly dropped my drink I was sipping on.

There she was standing there naked as the day she was born and without a care in the world that anyone could even see her. She wasn't trying to be sexy or nothing, but she just reaped sex appeal. Her beasts were perfect, not too big and not too small. I would have a wonderful time burying my face in between them.

She sat down and reached for something that looked like body oil and started to rub her body down. I knew I had to turn away and I had to stop watching, but even though I knew I was invading her privacy, I just couldn't stop.

"Are you going to get that are you going to stand there all night staring at the door?"

I pushed my favorite memory of her aside and open up the door. Tonight there will be one thing she's going to learn about me and that is I love the best of everything and I have to have just that. Now that she has gotten all my attention and I have tasted her sweet lips it was over with.

I made my mind up once I get her out of this situation. She will be my lady, but tonight I'm going to enjoy making love to her and make an imprint on her mind. Then she wouldn't want nothing else but for me to be laying deep up in her every night.

I opened the door still smiling because now it was time to put my plan into motion. I paid for the delivery and made my way back to my lady to be. Damn that sounded good. I'm going to lock that pussy down and tonight's just as good as any other.

Susan

As I patiently waited I thought about having a cigarette. I didn't see any ashtrays around so chances are he, or nobody else he knew smoked. Good thing I never made a habit to chain smoke, but when I got nervous I had to have my just due. I knew after this encounter I was definitely going to need a Newport.

Greg returned with the delivery and I could smell the aroma of something tasty. The scent wasn't a familiar one, but the dessert was going to be more to my liking.

He abruptly walked past me, "Be right back Hunny"

I smiled. "Please hurry I'm not used to waiting for what I want."

He returned 10 minutes later and reached out his hand to me. When I took his hand into mine, he said; "Right this way my Lady."

Rushing me through one door then another, a short turn and at the back of the house was a rather large indoor patio with sliding glass windows and doorway which led out to the pool overlooking the ocean. The scenery was beautiful, and the garden was well kept as if the gardener lived right here on the premises.

He led me out back off the patio to a table that he had set up rather nicely. I observed the decor, not bad for a bachelor I stated. He pulled out my chair as I took a seat he hurried over to his and sat. He reached in an ice bucket and pulled a bottle of red wine.

I watched as he poured a glass and handed it to me, and then poured a second glass. I felt myself getting wet. I lifted my glass up to my lips before saying, "Stealing a woman's heart must be your specialty."

He looked at me without a response. I reached over to his side of the table while extending my leg and put my foot up against his crotch. Lightly rubbing his penis, he reached down with both hands grabbing my toes in one wrapping the other around my foot with his thumb at the arch. As he was pressing and rubbing up, releasing and sliding down, I climaxed.

He looked into my eyes as he did at the crime scene and with conviction said, "If you're in a hurry to get to dessert, let's eat."

Just like that. I knew he wasn't a hard ass, but a man who was humble, modest and most of all knew when he had power, never to over step his boundaries. I don't know who the killers are, but right now they can sign me up because I would kill anybody to have this man.

As we ate, we indulged in small talk. As soon as we were finished he got up came around and slid my chair out. On my lap was a place napkin that he removed as I stood. Now stood face to face I couldn't believe how easily he used the napkin and wiped my lips ever so gently.

He walked me over to a place where there was a blanket laid out. There also were candles lit which flickered on every slight breeze that came by. Greg scooped me up and went down on the blanket to his knees. Holding me in his arms he never buckled or toppled over. I admired his strength.

He leaned forward laying me down with him above me partially, my eyes closed as his lips touched mine. It felt like a taste of Heaven that lasted 5 minutes, and then paused as we both searched for answers to questions that would never be answered.

I got a glimpse over his shoulder at the most beautiful sun setting I had ever laid eyes on. At that moment his legs slid between mine as mine opened wider. We touch lips, tongues, saliva. I'm fading fast into a blissful abyss of pure love...

Chapter 13

Greg

As she laid there under me I looked down into her beautiful face. I could so clearly see the full moon in her eyes. Her lips were shiny from our kisses. It only made me want to kiss her more. When I touched my lips to hers and deepened the kiss her arms went around my neck pulling me closer.

She moaned which only made me moan. I eased my hand behind her head and lifted it up higher so I could take her mouth fully. Her skin was hot to the touch. I could feel it through my shirt. It only made me want to touch her more. She didn't even pull away when I removed one of my hands and started running it down the side of her body. She loosened her grip around my neck to give me better access.

So I took that as an open invitation to do what I do best. There wasn't anything going through my mind but pleasing this beautiful woman under me. When my hand reached one of her breasts she sighed. It sounded like she has been waiting on my touch forever.

With her legs being wide open, it wasn't anything for me to get more comfortable between them. So I broke our kiss and started kissing down the side of her neck. I didn't stop until I was at the top of the shorts she had on. Her breathing was fast. Her heart rate was faster, but for all I know it could have been mine.

She lifted her hips up silently telling me she was ready for me to explore deeper. I was ready to explore. I was ready to deep sea dive all up in her treasure. Her body heat and her juices made a smell all on its own. I wanted nothing more than to take a drink.

I slide the shorts down her legs slowly enjoying the feel of her soft skin. Her moans increased as I opened her legs even wider so I could easily part her secret garden. She was already wet and her juices cover my fingers as soon as I opened up her silky folds.

She started to move with every touch I made. It was almost like she was begging me without words. If she only knew what that did to me she wouldn't be doing that right now. My manhood was pressing up against my pants; jumping as if it was yelling to be taking out.

I ran one of my fingers down the side of her silky wet folds. Then I eased it inside. She was warm, wet and it wasn't long before she started to move again. I pulled my finger out as I teased her. Then in its place was my tongue. I moved it across her clit slowly at first until I felt it harden even more. She was ready for me and I was ready for her, but I wasn't finished just yet.

Susan

His touch made my body quiver as his hands made their way down to my pleasure box; I knew he would feel my wetness. I was self-lubricated and ready to receive his jolly good fellow, take me, I'm yours my body screamed out.

I slid my hands under him reaching for his stomach. Going down further, I wiggle my hand inside his trousers reaching for his already stiff dick. As soon as I got my hands around it I slid my fingertips up and down his shaft. With my other hand I undo his belt, trousers button, and then finally his zipper. Down it went.

I removed my other hand and placed both hands at his sides, sliding his pants and boxers down over his firm butt and below his hips. His huge cock plopped down on my stomach. As his trousers lowered, so did I, until my mouth was right below the head of his hard pulsating dick. I stuck out my tongue and swiped it across the tip, tasting his pre'cum.

I placed my hand above his erected member and used my tongue to go up and down the shaft will delicacy so that he felt every brush. I inserted him into my wide open mouth and close down on it, taking him in deeper and deeper trying to reach his balls. I couldn't get that far, as he was so long and very thick.

He reached down and grabbed the back of my head holding it in place as he slid himself in and out of my wet drooling mouth.

"Relax Love."

He tilted my head back slightly and went in. I was waiting for him to pull back but, he didn't. Just further in until the head of is dick was in my throat and sliding down. I was amazingly shocked, breathing through my nose and didn't gag. He slid back out a little and then went back down even further until my lips met his body.

I stuck my tongue out and was able to get it on his balls and wiggle it as best I could. He pulled back up and all the way out. He turned around until we were in the 69 position. Putting his head between my legs and entering my jewel with his tongue, it felt like a thumb stroking in, out, and around, searching every possible detail as if it knew what it was looking for.

His legs slid apart, lowering his body to mine. I reached for his dick and began sucking again. My body arched up, moving from side to side, I moaned while still pleasing his hardness. His stamina wasn't at all questionable, but me on the other hand, I let out a big (ughhh) and squirted all that my body had to give.

At that point he placed his arms under me and around my petite frame; he came to his knees and lifted us both straight up off the blanket. We were still in the 69 as he stood he held me upside down. Licking, sucking, nibbling, teasing, and pleasing each other we continued.

Chapter 14

Greg

I slowly walked inside the house moving around objects that I knew from memory. Damn she was good she didn't miss a stroke as I moved to the bedroom. I took my time as I eased down slowly on the bed. I lifted her up higher so when I sat down there would be no problem. I love a woman that was down for anything. Most women would have stopped by now. Hell I haven't done that move since my college days.

Once seated on the bed I placed my face right back down on the sweetest pussy I ever tasted. I licked, sucked, and drank her up. I was afraid that if I stopped I would start to go through withdrawals from not having her in my mouth.

She sucked like a pro once she got used to my size and now she's deep throating it like the best of them. Only for a second I let my head fall back and just enjoyed her motion, but the entire time I had my fingers deep in that super wet pussy.

When I started moving my fingers in and out I felt her pussy tighten around my fingers. I knew then that she knew how to work her muscles. Just feeling that movement and her fire head I was about to cum. My man was hard as a rock and she knew I was close.

She tightened her mouth around me and started to suck harder. I buried my face back in her pussy and worked her clit like my tongue had batteries. All I knew I wasn't going to be the only one about to explode in a few seconds. I ran my teeth across her clit and I felt her intake of breath and I knew then I had her.

She released the grip she had on my dick only for a second before she gained control again. So I repeated it over and over again until I felt her legs beginning to tighten around my neck. I didn't stop until her pussy gave me the juices that I needed; then and only then I let myself go and exploded down her throat.

Susan

I felt his body loosen up and slide back, lowering my knees to the bed... The bed, I hadn't even realized we were inside. I rolled over to my back swallowing his creamy delivery and taking a breath of air. Crawling around to him, I nestled my head on his broad chest, and his masculinity.

I put my hand over his semi-hard thrill piece and firmly took hold, gently shaking it back to life. In seconds my head trailed my hand until I met the head of my household. I sucked it softly perking it right back up quickly. I straddled myself atop his cupid's arrow inserting his steadily growing penis into my soak and wet pussy, it slid in but with a tightness. I had never accommodated such a gorilla size of a man.

Before long he was in me and I was gripping his Johnson like a newborn on a tit. Gyrating my hips in multiple directions, side winding and deep stroke grinding him like there was no tomorrow. I came at least three times, once just getting it in, but stopped counting when his rhythm matched mine and then effortlessly took the lead.

I had to loosen up, spin around on him for a backwards down play to show him I'm not one to just easily lose control of a situation when the ball was in my court. I heard my cell phone go off to Tom's ringtone...

"you and I / doing things that dreams are made of / no lie no need to cry / it ain't magic it's love / I'm the hand / you're the glove / ... An old after dark erotica cut by a local artist called Brooklyn,

This was a song that Tom would always quote to me during every encounter. I pushed that out my mind as Greg just flipped me onto the bed and entered me from behind. I thought to let him get it in real good and before he splashed, pull up sliding him out and putting his massive banana into my ass... that may just hurt me way too much.

Chapter 15

Greg

My eyes started to roll to the back of my head as soon as she slid down on my man. She was extra tight and dripping wet. I felt her juices rolling down my legs as she turned and put that big ass in my face. I couldn't help but cuff her butt and give her cheeks a firm squeeze.

I loved the fact that her pace was not too fast. It was just right for a pussy that tight, but I felt like she was playing with me so I gripped her hips and really started hitting her cherry pie like it was the last dessert at the table. I could still feel that she was holding back so it wasn't anything else left for me to do but hit it from that back.

Yeah, she may try to run but that pussy can't hide. Plus I just love the way her sweetness just holds my man like a glove, but she didn't try to run. It was as if she was more into it this way. She matched my every stroke and I wasn't playing with the pussy at all.

Her moans were turning me on to another level, and every time I think she's getting close to overflowing on me she takes my strokes to another speed. She was acting like she was driving a six speed. I felt my balls hitting across her ass, because I was deeply inside of her and she was creaming like crazy. I was covered from the head of my man all the way down to the base. Damn she gave me another meaning for face down and ass up.

I think I'm in love with this woman. I'm going to try whatever it takes to get her crawling on her hands and knees to me.

I felt her tighten around me again and I couldn't help but throw my head back and roar. Oh yeah she is taking me to my limits and I never had a woman to do that to me before. I guess it's a first for everything.

My strokes didn't stop once I felt her explode and she was exploding like a volcano. Her juices were hitting me almost up to my chest, but I wasn't finish with her. I wrapped my hands around her hair and pulled her head up against me. I didn't leave any space between her juicy woman and my swollen man. Now it was time for me to take this shit into 6th gear.

Susan

I've been wined, dined, tossed, flipped, poked, stabbed, pull, pushed, and put to sleep all in 12 hours not including the two hour drive. After collapsing on his torso, with my legs between his with his dick still inside me, I don't remember if I either passed out or was surly exhausted from the workout.

My eyes opened, my arms stretched out and I yawn. Something didn't feel right... My head was on a pillow. Was I awaking from a dream of the greatest moment of my sexual life? I leaned up and looked around. Yes I'm in the right place no dream, but no Greg either. I reach over to the table where my cell was and touched the screen; oh great it's 10am, I'm sure Mr. Officer had to check in for work and get the evidence back to lock up before it becomes tainted making it inadmissible.

I have six missed calls, only one from H.K. I touched on that one and sent him a quick text. I put the phone down on the bed and leaned up. There was a bag sitting on a chair in the corner, oh good my things are here. I hopped up and saw a note safety pinned to the pillow next to me.

"Dear Sexy,

Thanks for being you and allowing me to be me. I feel our connection is a genuinely unique one that brought joy into my life. I went out for my daily morning jog as you slept, and when I returned you were still asleep. I watched you for a minute wanting to recap, but I let you rest and got one off in the shower. I know I shouldn't have said that but what the hell. I don't see any need to be shy..LOL..I went to the station and will return shortly, your things are in a bag on the chair in the corner. I left a kiss for you on your forehead please enjoy and I'll see you soon".

Sweet, this man doesn't miss a thing. I go for the bag, reach in for my laptop and charger. I set it up at the table on the patio out back and went back in. Walking into the bathroom, I grabbed a towel and wrapped it around me. I went back out to the patio picking up pieces of clothing leading back to the blanket

As I dropped every item into the center of the blanket a key had fallen out. I reached down to retrieve it, putting it on the chain around my neck. Damn I almost forgot about that. I quickly rolled up the blanket and headed back into the house. I dropped that off on the bedroom floor and went for a quick shower.

Sitting at the table I opened several files and got back to working on my case. Missing one more piece to the puzzle, I stare at a blank picture with a big question mark where the face should be... Who are you? I don't know yet but as sure as my name is Susan Williams, I will find out. You are messing with the wrong Sister, Mister.

An email notification pops up on my screen, I open it. No sender, just four words. "You are being monitored!"

WTF. I put my hand on my chest... OMG! I reached for a paper napkin on the table and draped it over the laptops camera. I never thought that someone could have been watching me so I went into the control panel and switched off the GPS. My next step was to go to Google and put in the info imprinted on the key.

Hmmm interesting... This key belongs to one of The Law Firm's accounts, a safety deposit box. I needed to retrieve the contents of that box fast. I was just about to log off when I heard the front door open.

Chapter 16

Greg

When I woke up this morning I tried hard not to wake Susan. She felt so good in my arms; I just wanted to lay here and hold her close forever. I eased from under her and put a pillow in my place. She pulled it close to her and sighed. I smiled because I knew I got a hold of that ass good. That came from months of watching and lusting after her. She just doesn't know she let that wolf out.

I wanted to wake her up but she looked so peaceful spread out all over the bed. So I headed for the shower. I haven't given my body a workout like that in months. I grinned once again as flashing of the night before surfaced. I stepped in the shower and let the hot water hit my muscles, but my most important muscle wouldn't relax because the scenes of Susan continue to flow; so I didn't waste any time reaching down and grabbing a hold of my monster. It wasn't long before I handle my business and headed into the office for a minute. It's still early so she should sleep for a while. I had to get the file back before someone noticed that it's gone.

When I walked through the door the first

thing I saw was Susan and so many emotions came over me. It felt like I was coming home after a long day at work. I never really had been a big family man being the only child growing up. I tried hard not to think about all the moving we did because of my father's career, but with this woman a sense of being home hit me like a brick and my body reacted before I was able to get control of it.

Now I'm standing here face to face with a woman wishing I knew where this road was heading between us. I walked over to her pulled her into my arms for a kiss and when I released her I asked, "So how long have you been woke?" She looked up at me with those soft brown eyes,

"I haven't been up that long, but we need to talk."

I followed her eyes as she looked over at her laptop.

"Don't tell me you tried to get on line Susan?"

"Yes but."

"Dammit Susan you shouldn't have done that." I didn't mean to yell but we weren't dealing with regular criminals here. "Go get your things. We have to leave." She stood there shaking. "Now dammit Susan get a move on it!"

Susan

I tried to explain that I disabled the GPS tracking system on it, but he's the officer here and knows more about this tech stuff than I do. So I jumped up and the towel slid off my body. He stood there barking at me but couldn't resist gazing at the cookie he took a bite out of just last night.

I walked over to where my things were and quickly slipped into a knee-high skirt, carnation pink blouse, and the matching blazer to the skirt. I reached down and grabbed my heals. He grabbed my hand and we rushed out the door. Out front was an unmarked squad car, his personal job vehicle I would imagine. I also thought that was good thinking on his part. Anyone chasing a police car has got to be insane, especially if it's crooked cops.

We got into the vehicle and without second glance pulled off, tires screeching. I can tell from how he handles a situation he has done some time in the military, Marines or Navy would be my guess. It was a two hour drive back to the city so I engaged in small talk.

"You know, I have been steadily seeing an old friend."

"Really?"

"Yes, he was married but..."

"But, but what?"

"Well we go back to high school. He went to NYU and I went to Yale. He got married because she got pregnant with twins forcing him to leave college and join the Army. I just had friends in college, nothing serious you know... books first. Then I went to law school and did my internship at The Firm where I'm currently working.

"That was a good career move for you, and to have had the same job this long shows dedication and loyalty."

"Yes, that's all good but what I'm saying is, I haven't been given the opportunity to settle down, and I think its high-time that I do.

"I see your point".

"Well, I'm sure by now we are both probably on the same page, but if not then we're definitely in the same book. I was just thinking, and this is just a hypothetical. Maybe after all this is over we can continue to see each other. I'm kind of getting used to having a personal bodyguard."

"Bodyguard... is that how you see me?"

"No not really, but you got to admit, it is kind of romantic in a roundabout way."

"I can see your point of view".

"Shit you do got me like Whitney Hoston in that movie with Kevin Costner."

He busted out in a laugh. "And do I come off as a white man too?"

"Oh goodness no; It's not that I have nothing against white men, but you do come across as a very protective husband."

"1. I'm just doing my job, 2. I was ordered by my Captain to meet with you so you could view the files and 3..."

`   "Was sleeping with me apart of your assignment too?"

"And 3 I have the hot's for you. It hasn't been long, but I wanted you from the first our eyes met."

I looked at the clock on the dash; we still had quite a bit of a way to go. I reached over and put my hand on his dick, he never took his eyes off the road, unless it was to look in the rearview as if someone was back there tailing us. I undid his zipper. He didn't even flinch. He grew right in my hand.

I leaned over into his area and put my head down. I knew most men had a thing for getting head on the highway but I couldn't imagine if any of them were on duty cops.

Well this was a first for me. I opened my mouth and went down on his big dick. I sucked it, teased it, twirling my tongue around the head waiting for its release when I heard the dispatch came across the car's radio...

"All cars respond to a "112" in progress at

Wells Fargo on 18th and Commonwealth Blvd".

Greg hit the siren and floored the pedal. "That's in my district, I need to be there", he mumbled.

Holding on to his stiffness, I gave it one last passion kiss and tucked him away.

"We will have to finish this later". I strongly agreed.

Chapter 17

Greg

Damn if Susan wasn't fucking with my head. What was she getting at anyway asking could we continue to see each other? If she thinks she was getting away that easily she would be sadly mistaken. I have tasted, sucked, fucked, and licked her. She wasn't going anywhere. Plus I already knew about that married dude that she was seeing, and believe me if she really knew how long I'd been watching her she would have me locked up for stalking.

My inside jumped as soon as her warm hands touched my man. I don't know why but as soon as she touched me I started to harden. My mind wasn't on sex right now but one touch from her and everything else went out the window.

I was riding on fumes. I don't know where to take her so I just drove with no destination in mind. That was until I heard the call that came over the radio. At least if I do a little work I could come up with something in the mean time to do.

In the meanwhile there's a hotel across the street from the bank so I will just check us in there until something else comes to mind.

"So are you not going to talk the rest of the trip back?" She asked.

"Susan I'm just thinking as I go sweetie just let me get my thoughts together." I said while looking in the rearview mirror.

"So you're running there to work and what am I supposed to do just sit in the car the whole time."

"Don't say crazy or stupid things Susan. You're too pretty and smart for that, but anyway I just came up with somewhere to take you."

She looked over at me. I could tell that she wanted to ask me where, but she didn't say nothing else. She just sat back and watched as we ate up the miles back to the city.

Once I hit the city limits I slowed down my pace a little. Hell we made it here in less than an hour. Susan had fallen asleep almost 20 minutes ago. She didn't wake up until we pulled to a stop in front of the Best Western.

"So this is your plan to have me cooped up here in a hotel while you out working?"

I reached for her hand and kissed it slowly.

"Baby I have to keep my face out here I don't want no one to link us together okay."

She sighed. "Yes okay come on."

I dropped her hand and got out the car. She was taking her time heading inside the hotel. I shook my head standing there with the door open waiting. The whole time her eyes were going back and forward across the street.

This was the perfect place. No one would think to look for her across the street where hundreds are cops are trying to stop a robbery. Her pace was slow and I could understand that. First she's cooped up at the beach house and now she has to be cooped up at a hotel. I could see she wanted to complain, but just from being around her this little time. I also could see that she knew when to shut up and go with the flow of things

Susan

I wasn't pleased with the outcome of this situation, but I also knew that I had to do what I was told. I might look like am touch, but inside I'm scared as a four year old child. I know that he's showing patience with me, but I am beginning to see the pressure of not knowing what's going on beginning to get the best of him.

He is a strong proud man, and I'm blessed to have him here protecting me, but I'm as stubborn as he is and just like he wants to get to the bottom of this so do I.

As he kissed me on the way out the door, I reached for the key around my neck.

"Take this; it's a key to a safety deposit box inside that bank.

"Where did you get this?"

"That's not important now, but I know it's a big piece of this case and probably why the bank is being robbed." As he took hold of the key, I looked in his eyes "I don't have anyone I can trust right now."

He looked at me "You can trust me baby girl." Then he gave me another kiss as he walked out the door.

It is best that I am not at the bank. I'm not in the right mind frame to be dealing with this right now. I walked over to the window and looked out.

At lease I feel safe right now. So I reached for my holster and removed my side arm placing on the dresser beside me. HK, what is he doing here? I reached for my cell and hit the speed dial.

"Hell, Susan where are you?"

"Close Boss."

"Thank God I thought..."

"I know but I'm safe right now. I have all the Intel we need on this case minus one big piece that I will have when the bank situation is resolved."

"Were you summoned here as well?"

"Summoned?"

"Yes, I received an email telling me there was a problem at the bank, some sort of embezzlement of company funds".

"It's a trap Boss; don't go in under any circumstances. Do you have a key to a safety deposit box in that bank?"

"Yes, I do. Do you know what this is all about Sue?"

"No sir I don't; not until I retrieve the contents of what's in that box. Do you have any idea what it may be?"

"No. My father gave the key to me when I finished law school and asked that I never reveal the contents unless deemed necessary."

"Well I think it's very necessary at the moment. A lot of people are dying for what's in that box. I have someone going in now to get what's in there, Sir stay where I can see you I'm coming to you now..."

Chapter 18

Greg

Once I closed the hotel room door I lifted my hand up and looked at the key Susan placed in it moments before. She really did surprise me. Did she really think I didn't know what was inside of that folder before I gave it to her, and what was missing when I took it back? I've been a cop too fucking long to be played with, but I had to see what she was up too.

Yeah I'm into her true enough, but I still have a dead lawyer on my hands, and also her life to protect. I needed to see which team she played for; because most people get betrayed by the most beautiful of women. I wasn't going to have my head turned by a pretty face and a banging body. When I heard the elevator sounded off I made a run for it. I was wasting to must time standing up here obsessing over Susan I have a job to do.

I stood in front of the hotel watching the cops going in and out. I looked around a few minutes more before I made my way to the officer in charge. I needed some details on what's going on.

As I was talking I continued to scan the area

trying to see if I could make out someone here that could have been at the last crime scene. Most sicko's like to watch the outcome of what they did. Then out the corner of my eye I saw a movement coming from the hotel.

When I left out there was an officer posted at the door and now he's gone. *"Shit,"* I said to myself when I saw Susan standing out front talking to some man. *"Dammit is she trying to get herself killed."*

"Excuse me." I said the officer and made my way back across the street. They were so deep into their conversation they didn't hear or see me coming up. I wanted to say there was a surprise look on Susan's face but something tells me she planned this hold thing.

She knew I would come back over here if I saw her standing out here. Was she trying to get my attention off the robbery or maybe she was trying to tell me something? I don't know but I'm damn show about to find out.

Susan

"OFFICER GREG?" I said, startled by his approach from my blind side. "This is my Boss, Mr. Karvell." The two shook hands.

"Excuse me, Susan may I have a word with you".

We stepped a few feet away from HK, "Yes Greg what is it?"

Trying to keep his composure, "What are you doing out here in the open?"

"I went to law school and studied law as my major and criminal science as my minor."

"Susan, what the hell does all that have to do with you being out here?"

"All I'm saying is that I have military training and am very capable of protecting myself. I know that you are the officer and I am a prosecuting attorney. I don't over step my bounds, but something tells me that I'm not the target. Call it a hunch or a fool's misconception, but I feel it in my gut"

He looked at me; "Susan this is stupid. I wish you just do as I say, but I see that you're not. So I'm going into the bank and you and I will discuss this later."

He reminded me of my father just then, when I would get a "B+ " on one of my grades.

"Yes Sir", I snapped back with a smile.

He stared at me a more moments before lifting his arm and motioned for two officers that were just standing around.

He walked away from me but he made sure I heard every word he said as he started barking orders to the officers;

"Watch them two until I get back and do not let them leave your sight". He never broke eye contact as he spoke. "If they have to use the bathroom, you're there to flush. If they need to take a trip to the moon, you are flying the space shuttle. If for any reason I return and they are not together side by side, I will have your badges on my desk understand me?"

"YES SIR", both rookies said in synch like Manilli Vanilli in concert.

A car pulled up and out steps the Captain of Police and the Chief of Police along with Anthony? Greg walks over to them and starts talking and pointing around. I can read lips, but his back is towards me. Now I see officers spreading out along the city block and more unmarked patrol cars arriving. Greg walks back over to me as a van pulls up with S.W.A.T on the side. A table and canopy tarp is being set up and phones.

"Sue, we have the men inside on the second floor with hostages, this may get ugly so please, you, and your boss wait inside the hotel lobby." He looks from me to the officers. "Officers please escort them inside".

He turns around to the new arriving officers and starts giving out orders; "I want two men each in every adjoining building on that side of the street. No one goes in and no one comes out."

As we get to the hotels front doors I turn and see him gearing up in the black riot suit S.W.A.T provided for him... I take it he's going in with them. This is his case for sure now and with something like this I know he's due for a promotion.

There I go with this feeling again that something's not right. I was sitting at the lounge with my boss when I asked for his cell. I switch the GPS on and called Anthony from his phone.

"Hello"

"Hello Tony it's me Susan, I'm calling from Harvey's cell lock the GPS signal in."

"Got it Sue, but what's this about?"

"We been down this road Tony, precautionary measures and do the same for my cell you already have the code."

"Got you."

Chapter 19

Greg

As I slipped into gear I took one last look and saw that Susan and her boss was heading inside the hotel lobby. Good I don't need to be worry about them when I'm trying to get to be bottom of this. I stood over to the side and watched as the head of the SWAT separated his men. I looked over at my Captain and he nodded his head in the directions of the SWAT team that went through the side entrance. So I followed suit.

Once inside I saw that the power had been cut off and we could hear people yelling and screaming that were struck inside the elevator. Hell at least they were safe. We move to the left side where the fire exit was located and started up the stairs.

Inside the stairwell we turned the lights on that were on top of our head gear. The only noise that we heard came from the women that were crying on the level above. The first man ahead pointed down letting us know that the robber's had the fire exit door half way open.

Everyone had their backs up against the wall ready to rush in when they heard shots going off, but the shots coming from the second level, they were coming from the level below. There must have men down there too. How many robbers were there? We had to take advantage of the situation.

We watched as the head man held his hand up holding up three fingers and as he dropped each finger my heart started to race. This is the part of my job that I love which I hardly get to do anymore. One by one each finger went down. Then just like that, he pulled opened the door with guns up and ready we rushed inside.

The hall way was clear when we stepped out. Guns pointing in every direction and the only thing I head from the Captain was "*Go find them now*." The units broke into teams of threes.

I walked with my eyes and ears opened trying to catch any noise or catch sight of anybody. My steps were slow and steady checking every corner I came across and that's when I heard it a small sound coming from the left side of the building. I held my fingers up and pointed in that direction.

Susan

Now that Tony has locked on to the GPS of HK I handed him his phone back. I felt very uneasy, but the hotel was quiet... no movement and that seemed kind of odd being the middle of the day. I shrugged it off as maybe the episode across the street has the attention of bystanders as well as patrons. Still feeling fatigue from the drive and the escapade from the night before, I remembered I hadn't had my cup off Joe.

"HK can you be a dear and get us some coffee, I have to use the ladies room?"

"Sure thing Sue, I can really use a shot of Brandy mixed in mine right now".

We stood and parted ways as the two officers looked confused. The elevator bell sounds as I walked into the door of the ladies bathroom, and I thought ok someone is awake around here. Once inside I saw that someone was utilizing one of the stalls so I stepped into the one next to it.

When I was done I exited and walked over to the wash sink and looked in the mirror. Wow girl your hair is a mess. The door opens slightly and the voice of the officer yells in.

"Is everything ok in there?"

"Peaches & Cream." I holla back. "I'll be out in a sec'."

I run my fingers through my hair and head for the door. As I walk out there was no sign of the officer, just the elevator door closing. I turn to walk toward the lounge and am grabbed from behind. As I reach for my side arm... damn. The holster is empty; I had taken it out upstairs and left it on the table.

The assailant grabs my arm and twists it behind my back. Shoving me toward the elevator, I see three other men headed toward HK and the officer. He turns and reaches for his gun, but is shot once in the chest. He falls and HK drops both cups of coffee.

One gunman walks over to HK as another walks over to the wounded officer struggling to breathe. He was wearing his vest, thank God.

The gunman looks down at him, aims and shoots. I want to close my eyes but I can't. I scream as I watch the officer take one to his head. They grab HK and lead him toward the elevator. The one who had a hold on me pulls me on the already opened elevator and the doors close. It's going up. I thought the others and HK would be right behind. The elevator stops at the top floor and we enter into the staircase walking up one flight to the roof.

Out on the roof is a helicopter with one man in the pilot's seat. We get onto the helicopter and it takes off. I thought, *"Oh my God, what about HK? What are they going to do with Him?"* Just then a black cotton like bag is thrown over my head and tied. I try to struggle but am forced into handcuffs and shackles are placed around my ankles.

Chapter 20

Greg

I stood still with my back up against the wall watching the movements from that other room. The door was half open and three masked men are blocking the door with machine guns. I looked back at my team and held up my hand giving them the count of three. I love the element of surprise.

When I looked back inside I saw that one of the bank employees had made eye contact with me. I put my finger up against my lips and lower my hand down telling him to drop down on his knees. With gun in hand and sweat running down the side of my face I slowly walked inside the room.

More and more people noticed what was happening as I walked up behind one of the robbers and used the butt of my gun and hit him in the back of his head.

When he dropped the other masked men turned around and saw a room full of SWAT pointing red beams at their heads and chests.

"That's right drop you weapons slowly." I said aiming my gun at the man closest to me, but he didn't move. Instead he turned his weapon on me.

One of the officers behind me yelled out. "
All of you get down on the ground and put your
hands on your head"

Everyone dropped except the two masked
men. Now let's see could they pull someone in
front of them for coverage.

I shouted out, "Now I asked nicely once but
the next time I ask you it will not be so sweet. I
said put your fucking guns down now."

Now the room was filled with SWAT. The
people inside were scared and the women made
sure we knew it. The sound of their crying was
echoing across the room. You could hear their
teeth clapping together because the
fear was so thick inside the room.

Finally they noticed there was nowhere to
run and dropped their guns. It was like the two
masked men read each other's minds. As one laid
down on the floor he said aloud, "Fuck this I didn't
come here to die today."

Susan

The chopper was descending and the ride seemed over an hour long but actually was around twenty minutes after takeoff. That's probably about 30 minutes by car. I'm telling you fear makes a twenty minute ride seem like forever.

I had a hundred things going through my mind. I couldn't even remember if I put my cell on vibrate or not, but if it went off they would take it for sure. So far they hadn't bothered to search me.

As we landed my shackles was loosened and I was pulled to my feet and led off onto the platform of yet another roof. Once inside the black hood that covered my head was removed and the room was dark with one dim light that hung overhead. I could hear the helicopter leaving.

The man that led me to this dungeon said; "Here she is boss."

"Good, go meet the others and tell them to set up for phase 3." The door closed and locked. The voice spoke out to me. "I suppose you're wondering why you are here? Well there won't be any chance for a Q&A session, but I will tell you this... You were in possession of something I needed. Now you are not. Your cop friend has it now and soon he will be walking out the bank with it and I will take it from him. Your boss,. hmm I guess you don't know as much about him as you should, but if you somehow manage to survive, you will discover a great deal. Now, have a seat you are going to be here a while."

"That still doesn't tell me what you want with me if I don't have whatever it is you are looking for, but if it's about that $50,000 I can get that for you from my account.

"My my. You think I have men in a bank for just that? As I said, Greg has what I want and you are the link to be sure he hands it over if he wants you to live. I will have someone bring you something to eat and drink, good day Susan." The door opens; closes and the sound of the locks echo though the room.

I reached in my pocket and grabbed my phone. Shit, no signal. That's why I wasn't searched. This place must be re-enforced with steel. But they aren't smart enough; the GPS will give the last location before signal transition ended. Now I just have to wait, hurry Greg please.

Chapter 21

Greg

With guns pointed the men lowered their weapons. "That's right nice and slow gentlemen." I said as I walked up beside them and kicked the weapons out of reach. "You get down on your knees." He dropped down on his knees facing the employees. "Now get down on your stomach. You to mister get down on your fucking knees."

It wasn't long before the room was clear out and the employees were checked and released. I was on my way to the safe deposit box when I received a phone call.

"Sgt. Brown here." I said into the phone.

"Yes, Sgt. Brown I think you have something that I want." I pulled my phone away and tried to look at my caller ID but the number came back block. "There is no need trying to see where I'm calling from what you need to be doing is giving me what I need before I kill this pretty little lawyer." Then the phone went dead.

I looked around but everyone seems to be busy clearing out the bank. My mind went to Susan so I headed out the front of the bank and that's when I saw crime scene tape around the front of the hotel.

"Fuck." I said to myself and ran across the street.

Once I got on the scene I saw that one of the officers I left as guards had been shot dead right in the hotel lobby and the other one was found dead inside the men bathroom.

I took the elevator up to the floor our room was located on. I had to check and see at least if she was being held in our room. As soon as I stepped off the elevator I saw that our room door was open and police officers were standing guard outside the room door.

When I walked in the FBI agent was standing inside questioning someone. Our eyes locked and he excused his self.

"Greg, Susan called me and told me to lock onto her and her bosses GPS, and it's a good thing that she did because right now we are tracking them as we speak."

"Susan called and told you that but why? She was supposed to be safe here." I looked at the agent and I could tell that he was concern for Susan.

"Susan always has her way no matter the case so when she calls me and tell me to do something dammit I do it. She didn't give me a reason she just said something didn't feel right, and she was right."

"It's all my fault I shouldn't have never brought her here."

"This is not your fault Greg." The agent was cut off by the ringing of his phone. "Hey what you got."

Susan

All I saw was a desk, a chair and no windows; no clue as to where I am being held. I can see the shadow of a single pair of footprints approach the front door. "Click" and it swung open. Two men walk in dressed in all black, one stood over by the door as the other one came in carrying a bag from Wendy's. He placed the bag on the table and walked out, locking the door behind him.

I walk over to the bag and dig inside, a big classic with fries and a chocolate smoothie. "You got to be kidding me" I said out loud, where they do that at. I threw that shit on the table. I hadn't eaten fast food since high school.

I sat back down in the chair staring at my cell. I thought about playing one of the games that comes on the phone but my mind couldn't focus on anything but Greg. These people were serious and seem to have men in every department of law enforcement. I sure hope he follows the trail and has this pretty much figured out before he comes rushing here, because they are always two steps ahead of us.

What about poor old Harvey? I couldn't help but wonder why they separated us and where he is being held. I put my cell back in my pocket, as my mind returned right back on Greg.

I don't think they are going to be coming

back in here anytime soon. I took off my jacket and relaxed a little. Images of my new found partner of love flash before me. I rub a hand up inside my inner thigh as I was getting close to my jewel I can feel the heat it holds by just thinking about the thickness of his woman pleaser.

Now more images of the night from the silhouette shadow on the balcony start to flash before me. I couldn't help myself as I started to get horny. I put my middle finger on tip of my clit and stroke back and forth. The more images that flash the faster I start to rub. The more I rub the more images I see of Greg. This has got to be the one. I never found myself in this much heat over a man I just met. The chemistry felt right from the beginning.

Two fingers slide in me as I lean my head back and pleasure myself. My eyes roll back then open slightly. "What the fuck?" I lifted my head back up and looked up toward the corner of the room. I see it clearly now A Black Ops camera. That is only military issued and I bet if I could get up there to examine it that would be exactly what it reads.

I pull my fingers out as I started to get control of myself. The door unlocks and swings open. One man comes in and closes the door behind him.

"You look good on camera, and even better in person. So tell me pretty lady does all the excitement turns you on, or are you ready for some side action."

"Are you serious? I think you better go before your boss comes back and finds you laying on the floor."

"Oh, well look what we have here, a feisty sassy little lawyer." He laughs. "Seeing that today will be your last, I think I will just help myself and have a taste of your honey pot."

He walked towards me still running off at the mouth turning me off and disturbing the groove I was in. I didn't rise from my seat as he approached me and started fiddling with my hair. He leans over me reaching down grabbing one of my breasts and squeezing. I grabbed his wrist twisting his arm while standing and I turned to face him chest to chest.

"Is this what you want?" I asked as I put my lips on his and kneed him in the groin.

As he buckled over I released his wrist and send my open palm flying into his face shoving his nose into his head. I grabbed his arm spinning him around and bending it up his back walking him to the door.

He's screaming, "You broke my nose bitch. Get off of me, I'm going to kill you bitch."

I rammed his head into the door and gave it two kicks. As it opened up I shoved him out with a thrust and pulled the door to a close. He's pissed, but won't come back bothering me anymore.

I reached for my cell, 6 hours and still no rescue, where are they, what's going on out there?

Chapter 22

Greg

My mind went over the facts as I stood there waiting as the agent talked on the phone. I was beyond nervous I needed to know where my lady was. That's right I'm not a shamed of saying it. That's my girl and I'm going to find her even if it kills me. I don't like not being in control and I couldn't keep standing here doing nothing.

"Greg we picked up on Susan's GPS and she's about 30 to 45 minutes away from here."

"Then let's go. Why are you still standing there?" I could tell that he had more to say but was looking for a better way to say it. "Dammit man that's your friend too what is the problem?"

"It's not that simply that's the problem." Tony said while looking away for a second.

"What do you mean? Where is she?" He took me by the arm and walked into another room. I knew for a fact then that he couldn't trust anyone either.

"Look Greg her GPS puts her right in the middle of one of our military bases and you already know we just can't go walking up on them. We have to do this the legal way or those MF want let us nowhere near her."

"Damn I can't believe this. Okay I work from my end and you work from yours and let's get this done. I don't want her thinking we just left her out there to the wolves." I said shaking my head how much worse could this get.

"I couldn't believe this I mean I knew this was way up the ladder when it came to the people involved but the damn military too. What the hell are those people trying to hide?"

At that moment I pulled the safe deposit key out my pocket and realized that I forgot to check it. It wouldn't take that long to find out. I knew then that I had to see what was so important that they were killing people for it.

"Give me a second I think I may know why?" I said turning around and headed back over to the bank.

Traffic outside has returned back to normal and people started going on with their everyday lives like nothing never happened just hours ago. When I opened the banks doors and stepped inside most of the officers were gone so this was a good time to slip by unnoticed.

The path leading to the vault was clear so I didn't waste any time walking through the first set of doors; as soon as I put the key inside the locked safe deposit box my cell phone rings.

I pulled it out my pocket cussing the whole time but before I could even say hello someone started talking.

"This is Greg I hope." An irritated voice asked.

"This is him and who is this?"

"It's not important." There was a short pause. "What is important is if you want to save your pretty lawyer friend here. Now if that's true then I need for you to take the key out of the box. Do we understand each other?"

"Yes I understand."

"Now slowly I want you to pull that key out and put it somewhere nice and safe until I'm able to get it from you. As you can see I have eyes everywhere and I will know if you or anyone else comes close to that box. And Greg don't try me because I want think twice about snapping this pretty little lawyer's neck." Then the line went dead.

Fuck. Now I'll never know what the hell's in that box. We need to get clearance for that base and we need to get it now. There is no way in hell I'm turning over this key.

It took me a minute to make it back to the hotel because I was too busy trying to see who was watching me. When I walked back inside the hotel room the agent saw my expression and followed me into the bedroom.

I stood there with my back to him for a second before I turned around and started to fill him in on the phone call I had just received, and when I finished he got a call clearing us to infiltrate to military base. I couldn't help but think that was just too damn easy.

Susan

I'm sitting here in this dungeon trying to wrap my mind around plots, schemes, scenarios, and people tied in... dead and alive, but I'm still coming up with nothing. Greg keeps entering my mind, but my mood is lost now. My gut instincts tell me something still ain't right.

(TOM)... His name just pops up just like that. Someone from his Unit called me to tell me of his passing, not unusual but he was married so the wife yeah, but why did he leave a message for me? And gee, they were supposed to get back in contact with me today, but... I'm down and out at the moment.

Hmmm, I kept notes on my laptop following the list of events. I don't have a signal, but I can still work offline through Google and ICloud. I need to try and piece this puzzle together.

I start in right away, but still the contents of that safety deposit box are the biggest piece that's missing.

(RECAP)

Anderson Levi: on trial for killing his wife.

Tom Bennitt: killed overseas in Iraq?

Jack Palaski: killed in his car at a red light.

Harvey Kavelle: missing just as I am.

Ok what's the connection? What are you not seeing Sue... think.

Chapter 23

Greg

Anthony and I decided it was best to keep this new information between the both of us. We couldn't afford for anyone else to get hurt. So one by one we slipped out from the hotel trying our best to keep as many eyes off of us as we can. We couldn't trust anyone and that includes the FBI and the police departments.

I walked out of the side door of the hotel and Anthony was parked there with his black Crown Vick running. When I got inside the first thing he asked was,

"Did anyone see you leave?"

I grinned because everyone that was left inside eyes were glued on Anthony so it was easy for him to slip right passed them.

"No I don't think so they were too busy watching you."

Anthony laughed. "Yeah no wander I felt like someone had been watching me all day. Okay, from my understanding Susan is right in the middle of this and she didn't even know it. From the information that I came across that the trial she is working on now is tied into the trial Jack was working on, but this goes deeper than that."

"What you mean by that?"

I had to ask because if he was thinking what I was thinking then we needed to get Susan out of there as soon as possible. Even if those people get their hands on this key, Susan is dead anyway.

Then it came to me, "Anthony pull into this Home Depot I need to run inside for a second." He gave me a crazy look but he didn't say anything just pulled inside and stopped right in front of the door. "I know you have things going through your mind right now but I'll explain when I get back out"

I got out and walked through the sliding glass doors and headed for the area they make keys. Now I think I know why getting access to where Susan was being held is so easy. They're going to want to exchange this key for Susan. Why didn't I think of that earlier? I was in and out in no time. Anthony gave me that look as soon as my but touched the car seat.

Soon as I was about to tell him what I though was about to happen my cell rang again. I looked at the caller ID and the number was blocked.

"It's him again Anthony." I said as Anthony hit the gas.

"I see you're running late Greg I told you no games." The caller said.

"Running late and how you know where I'm headed"

"I see you taking me for a joke maybe I need to go and play with your pretty lawyer. She is a nice looking woman." He laughed into the phone.

"Don't you fucking touch her!" I yelled.

"Then you have 15 minutes to be sitting outside that base with the safe deposit box key and if you don't make it. I don't have a problem getting between her legs and going a few rounds." He hung up.

I could tell that Anthony had a good idea what had taken place on the phone. No words were said as he started hitting a record speed of 125 miles an hour trying to make it to the base before something happened to Susan.

Susan

I started getting sleepy sitting here trying to piece together past events. Then it hit me. HK has a twin sister who has a son... Tom. O'Riley Benson who's on trial for killing his wife, he plead innocent saying masked men in all black entered his home during the night while they slept. He was awaken by a noise and tried to fight them off. They killed his wife before fleeing.

His wife was the sister of Tom. Jack was killed because he stumbled onto the truth which is the connection of the deceased. Everyone alive who stood a chance of inheriting the contents of that safety deposit box is ending up dead. The only thing missing now is who is behind it all, and the masked men in black can answer that question.

I bet it's the same two who had been following me all day yesterday. "Click click," the front door unlocks. I slid my cellphone into my back pocket. The same two men who been here the whole time entered the room.

"Let's go, someone is here to see you".

I stood and made my way toward them. Stopping short of them, I looked at the one with the bandages on his face and asked;" How's your nose?" He didn't comment.

As I walked out the room I said to the two men, "Keep your hands where I can see them and nobody else will end up in bandages."

They both smirked as if I didn't know they had planned to do away with me the first chance they get. We get outside I followed close behind one of them as we went from the building into a hanger. A military base?

This goes even deeper than I thought.

"Have a seat until all parties arrive".

I look around and started to take a head count. Okay there are two men with me, the same pilot from earlier that brought us here. I continued to scan the area and saw two more men on the ground, over by the helicopter, and two on the overhead catwalk. As I could see all the men were armed and very alert, which could only mean that my people are on their way. This is going to be a tricky sticky situation, and I only hoped that they came prepared.

Chapter 24

Greg

When we pulled to a stop in front of the gates that lead to the base that's when we realized that this was one of the closed military bases that the government closed earlier this year. No wonder gaining access was so easy. No one was here.

Anthony continued to sit. Not showing any signs that he was about to make a move anytime soon.

"Why are you just sitting here for?" I asked him. He could tell that I was getting impatient.

"Greg your impatience isn't going to do nothing but get us both killed. We just can't walk up in there like that. Plus it's what they want anyway. Just think about who in their right mind would leave the main gates open to a military base."

I closed my eyes and dropped my head back into the seat. It gave me a second to really think.

"No one would." I said.

"Damn right no one so what you have in mind before we go on this suicide mission?"

I ran my hand down my face which was a habit of mine and if Anthony would have known me better he would have knew right then that I didn't have one damn clue as of what to do next.

"Okay what kind of gear you have on you?"

Anthony opened up the car door and headed for the back of the car hitting the button and the trunk popped open. I could see the look on Anthony face once he scanned the inside.

"All I have is two vests, one double barrel, and a M4."

I came and stood beside him grabbing the double barrel and the belt that came with it. Then I pulled out and checked both of my .45 Glocks.

I jumped when I heard a voice behind us.

"So do you guys need an extra hand or are you two too busy playing Batman and Superman." Charles said slapping me on my back.

"Dammit Charles you scared the hell out of me. What you doing here?"

"I called him when you were inside Home Depot." Anthony said as he picked up the M4. "I didn't know what we were walking into, and it was just the two of us you know."

"Well I got a few more things over here so let's get a move on it we don't have all day to play bad cop – good cop with these motherfuckers."

"I see you got jokes today Charles." I said as I felt a little of the weight lifted off me. I feel a little safer than I did five minutes ago that's for sure. We walked over to Charles car and grabbed a few more rifles and headed through the gates.

Susan

Call it instincts, but there goes my gut again... they're here. I can feel the strong vibe of Greg every time he is close by. Now I know that the time is near that I will be making my move soon. I have to try and take out both of the two black suits but keep them alive. The one I wounded earlier shouldn't really be a problem.

Wait what's happening now. The two by the helicopter walks over.

"Slight change of plans gentlemen, they won't come in and we can't just as we'll threaten to kill the girl. They're here so once they come through the gates we will meet them outside".

"What about them guys up on the catwalk"?

"They're coming down now and will meet up with us outside".

"Surveillance shows that it's only three of them, so we won't need the element of surprise".

"Once outside you two stay with the girl as originally planned, far off to the left. You know what you have to do, but don't do a damn thing until that key is in my hand and I have clarified that the serial number on it is a match. If anything goes wrong kill that bitch and get your asses back to the helicopter".

They talked like I wasn't even there. It was just like men to think they have all bases cover just because they out number someone. We start to make our way toward the hanger doors and outside. I could see three figures walking up and spreading out six feet apart from each other.

An old army offense move to confuse multiple trigger men incase gunfire erupts. Smart move. Anthony knows me well, as soon as I see the hand off; he knows I will make my move. Hopefully he explained that to Greg and the other guy.

Chapter 25

Greg

We walked through the gates like the scene on the movie "Bad Boy's". I could feel eyes on me everywhere but I was trained for this kind of shit so this didn't faze me.

Anthony made it clear that Susan could protect herself but all she needed to do was be able to get free. I knew there was something special about her.

The space between Anthony, Charles, and myself got wider the father inside the base we went. We were making sure we could cover all corners without having someone attacking us from behind.

Once we were halfway inside we stopped and I yelled out, "This is as far as we going until I see the girl."

One on the men in a dark suit grabbed Susan by her arm and tried to push her down to the ground, and that's when she begins to fight and that was our chance to strike.

Shot's started coming from all directions. So I aimed at the one closest to me which was the one that was up high on the platform. I aimed dead center firing once giving him a head shot. He dropped as I take aim at another one.

Someone else walked up to Susan pulling her up off the ground and put his gun to the back of her head, that's when all shots stopped.

The masked man started to speak, "Now that I have your attention." He hit Susan across the head and her eyes start to roll. "Give me the fucking key or the next time I touch this bitch, it will be a shot to head not a little love tap."

I gave Charles a look and lowered my rifle and walked slowly with my hands up. I knew I had to give the key to him for the return of Susan.

As I walked I saw that half this man power is lying dead on the ground. So if I just give him the key we all may just walk out of this alive. When I got close enough I reached out my hand showing him the key.

"Fair exchange the key for her do you understand."

I could tell from the look on Susan face she was still a little shaken for the knot hat was forming on her head, but she still didn't show any signs of fear.

"Yea I got you. Now you," the man in black said as he started to push Susan forward, "pretty little lawyer get the key from your boyfriend now." He pulled her back close to him as I gave her the key.

I had a close eye on Susan as she handed it over to him. Just as fast as she put the key in his hand was just as fast as he pushed her away. I watched with fear in my heart as he aimed and shot.

Susan

Once I got the key in my hands my first instinct was to protect it. We needed that to get into that box, but I looked at Greg, dead into his eyes and they read "no". I handed it over and before I could react I was shoved to the ground.

I could hear the sound of his gun going off and in my mind I'm screaming, "Oh my God I'm hit." But it missed me by inches.

Anthony returned fire but he also missed him as he took off running. The other men started shooting covering him as he made his getaway.

Greg came running over to me.

"Sue, Sue!" he screamed out, "Are you ok".

"Yeah he missed me."

"Come on, let's get out of here".

He helped me up off the ground while Charles and Anthony gave us cover as we made our way back to them. The sound of shooting stopped and all I heard was the sound of the helicopter as it made its way into the air.

I yelled out," Damn it, they got the key are headed for the bank.

"Not if we get there first, let's go". Greg said as he grabs my hand and made a run back to the cars.

Once we were safely in the car Greg showed me the key.

"But I just gave him that key." I said looking confused.

"No, what you gave him is a copy."

Both cars sped back to the bank with lights flashing the whole way. As the cars pulled to a stop, doors opened and one by one we ran inside.

Anthony stopped the first bank employee he saw and requested the bank manager as the men flashed their credentials.

The bank's manager walked up and asked, "Is everything alright." He eyed them. "Is this related to the recent robbery, because nothing was taken?"

"Yes, everything is just fine, but I need you to take us to the vault". Greg replied trying his best to ease his mind.

We watched as the manager ran back into his office to get the security key.

"Right this way gentleman," then he looked toward me. "Ma'am".

We followed him into the vault, and he placed his key into the lock on the left. He looked at Greg and instructed him to insert his key on the right. The manager told Greg that they both needed to turn their keys at once. As we heard the safe deposit door unlock. We held our breath as the manager pulled it open.

Greg reached in and pulled out the box. His eyes went from me to Tony. I could see the truth was about to be let out with just the turn of those two keys. We all walked over to the table and watched as he sit it down. It felt like hours passed instead of seconds. Greg lifted up the top and then looked back at us as he reached inside.

Chapter 26

Greg

The room was quiet and my hands were almost shaking. I could see that everyone eyes were glued trying hard to see what was inside that box.

"Can you believe this?" I said.

"What the hell!" Susan grabbed a hold of my arm. "I went through all of this shit for that?"

I looked from Susan to Anthony and I was about to reach my boiling point. "This has to be some kind of game. It has to be." I said placing the lid back on the empty box. "There is no way in hell they beat us here first. Did anyone else ask to see this box?" I asked the bank manager.

"No sir, no one else has been here."

The manager waited on what to do next.

"Thanks sir but that would be all." I said taking Susan by her arm and leading her out of the vault.

"I been followed, kidnapped, and shot at all for an empty box and where the hell is HK at anyway? Have you located where they was holding him at?"

I turned to Anthony giving him the eye letting him know that he needed to fill her in on what happened to HK. I think she been through enough for one day.

"I'll let Anthony tell you all about that okay baby. I'll be right outside if you need me."

The last thing in the world I want to do is see her hurt. The outcome of this whole thing is crazy and it doesn't seem like we no closer than we were at the beginning.

Charles was still waiting outside the bank when I walked up to him. Before he could ask me what was in the safe deposit box I put my hand up to stop him in mid-sentence.

"Before you ask me what was so important in that safe deposit box that was worth killing for I'm just going to come straight out and tell you. There was nothing inside that box!"

"What! If that's true Greg then this is far from over."

Susan

Greg walked outside, and I could tell he was furious more than he was confused. I was just as confused as he was. Then Anthony told me HK didn't make it out the hotel. There was a struggle and he was shot.

"You know HK Sue, it was only moments after we were informed that his people came and removed his body. They are going to have a private service for him after cremation".

"That's it?"

"Well my orders came from higher up to let the body go".

Damn, now what am I supposed to do?" I asked him.

"With the evidence collected, there are sufficient grounds to drop the charges on your case".

"Yes but there are a lot of people in that evidence we have to bring down and most won't even go to jail without knowing what this was all about. If only I knew what was in that box in the first place."

We walked outside still deep in conversation.

"You need a ride home.

"No Greg will take care of me."

"Ok, I need to get back to the office and put

in my report. I'll make sure you get a copy for trial". He says as he gave me a light kiss on my cheek.

"Thanks Tony."

I walked over to Greg still with a thousand questions going through my mind

"Are you ok Hunny?"

"Yes I'll be fine."

"You need to get that head of yours looked at".

"I know but not before I go retrieve my side arm and laptop from the hotel room.:

We walked across the street to the hotel. As soon as we walked through the front doors the first thing I saw was the outlines of the officer that were slain and where HK was supposedly shot and killed. I held my head down as we walked onto the elevator and that's where I collapsed.

Greg caught hold of me, stopping the doors from closing he yelled out to officers in the lobby, "Hey get the paramedics in here now."

I was coming to when I was being placed on a gurney and hustled out to a waiting ambulance still on the scene. While I'm being rushed to the ER the medics take my vitals listening to my heart. He looks at me and smiles.

Greg barks at him with conviction, "Does this look like a matter to be glee over?"

"No Sir, it's just that..."

"Just what son, spit it out".

"Well Sir, Ma'am, the problem is with all that's been going on today I was wondering when was the last time you ate?"

"Oh God, I haven't ate today."

"I could tell ma'am. Your sugar was a little low but the knock on your head didn't help things either."

Greg looked into my eyes deep and hard as his lips went into a shiver then cracked a big smile as he wrapped his arms around me.

"Don't scare me like that no more baby."

I put my arms around his neck and whispered into his ear, "Oh baby I want and thank you for taking care of me. You will never know how much I love you.

Chapter 27

Greg

I smiled when she said that she loved me and deep down I believed that I loved her too. I felt that it was only right for me to voice how I feel also.

"Susan baby I'm glad that you were okay, and that it wasn't anything too serious, because I don't think I would be able to handle if anything happened to you. I love you too."

When we arrived to the hospital it wasn't long before she was checked in and seen by the doctors. Once we were alone all I wanted to do was hold her; so I pulled her close. I closed my eyes and enjoyed the feel of her until she moved away.

"Baby we still have to get my things out of that hotel room."

I kissed her softly, "I make a call and get everything dropped over here. I know there are still a few officers left at the crime scene, but I want you to stop thinking about all that and start thinking about feeling better."

She smiled and laid back on the hospital bed. She looked so exhausted and all I wanted to do was take her home, run a hot bath, and then make love to her until she fell asleep in my arms.

"Don't worry about that baby I will take care of that right now."

She didn't say anything else and I knew that she had fallen asleep. I ran down to the cafeteria and picked her up a small chicken salad, a bowl of fruit, and a bottle of water. She was still asleep when I arrived back to the room so I stepped out and gave Charles a call.

"Hey I'm over at Peachtree General Hospital with Susan its nothing serious. I just wanted to fill you in, and also tell you that I will be in the office first thing in the morning to fill out my report."

"Well that's cool as long as you get in here tomorrow. I need that paperwork, and tell Susan that I hope that she feels better."

When I ended my call I couldn't help but think that so much had changed in my life since I met Susan. Yes it's been some drama, but that is what made being with her so exciting. When I opened her room door she was sitting up getting ready to eat.

Susan

I woke up and saw that Greg had been nice enough to go and get me something to eat. He is a good and caring man and I can't see myself letting him go. I don't think no one was more relieved than I that everyone got out of that situation safe. I hoped this mess was just about over.

Two officers arrived not long after I was discharged and ready to go. I was given a prescription of Percocet for the pain and something to help me sleep. The officers explained to Greg that the Captain had placed them on detail until he headed back to the office in the morning.

The two officers agreed to follow us over to my place so I could grab a few things. We left the hospital heading home.

When we arrived at the condo's we parked on the street, and I remembered that my car was still parked at the restaurant that Greg and I met up at. I wanted to say something about it but I knew he had enough on his mind for one day.

We took the elevator up to my place as the officer's posted up out front. I couldn't help but think was all of this necessary. I mean maybe it was over.

"Greg do you think the patrol is really necessary?"

"It can't hurt to be safe Susan, and this will help a lot if this isn't over yet."

I gathered up a few things, walked over to my desk, and grabbed a notepad. I scribbled down a note for the moving guys that I would be contacting later to move my things to storage.

I didn't feel safe here anymore so I didn't see any reason to stay. I loved this condo and it had been home for years, but it saddened me to know I had to give it up for reasons of the unknown.

Greg stood there waiting patiently as I said goodbye to my home. He knew I was a little emotional because he could see the sadness in my eyes. This was going to take some getting use to.

I walked over to him teary eyed and he held out his hand. I took it maybe a little too tightly as we headed for the door. Once he opened it and stepped out I followed. I turned and took one last look at my past as I closed and locked the door behind me.

Chapter 28

Greg

It's funny now that I had time to think about everything. How I fell for Susan just by peeking at her from one building to the next. I would think that someone with her education and background would think twice about getting involved with someone that had been watching her for months, but not Susan.

No, she is so trust worthy of everyone and that's what might end up getting her hurt or killed. Now she's standing looking out of my balcony window into her apartment. I had flashes of her with tears in her eyes as we were leaving. God I hated seeing her in pain. Just like now I could tell she had a thousand things on her mind.

I walked over to her and pulled her close. Her back was to me and I laid my chin down on top of her head.

"What are you thinking about, my sexy woman?"

I looked in the glass and saw that she was watching me.

She gave a little laugh "I was thinking about how far we came from playing those little sex games into what we have now."

I didn't say anything for a moment "And what do we have now Susan?"

I asked as I turned her around to face me. I had to see her face when she finally opened up to me without all the danger in the way, standing before her only the man that I am.

Yes I know that she said that she loves me. Maybe she said that in the heat of the moment, but I meant every word I said concerning her. I love Susan and I don't love easy and I want to spend the rest of my life showing her just how much.

Susan

Looking down at what is about to become my former place of residence, a feeling came over me. It was a warm feeling whereas most would be alarmed. Call it a pretty good judge of character or something I don't know, but what I do know is this. What could have easily been a stalker turned out to be Prince Charming, and I mean that in every sense of the term.

In thunder, lightning, and midnight rain, Cupid came to visit, and not only did I cross paths with Mr. Right, he saved my life.

Greg walks over to where I am and puts his arm around me.

"What are you thinking about"? He asked as he turned me to face him.

I was always taught some things are better left unsaid, and so without words I nestled my head on his chest and ran my hand up his leg.

"On the way from the beach house I was in the middle of something. I would like to finish what I started."

"Only if I am allowed to participate, I hate sitting around twiddling my thumbs".

"Oh, I have a feeling you'd be doing more than that."

I unbutton his shirt and peel it off his warm body and then moved on down to his slacks. I watched as they slide down to his ankles.

He undressed me first with his eyes, then physically, one piece of clothing at a time. There I stood standing there naked and bear as he continued to eye me.

I go down to my knees and placed his growing erection in my mouth. Slowly, tenderly, passionately... I suck his harden muscle. Taking it in it inch by inch until its deep in my throat just the way he showed me, just how he likes it.

I reach one hand up and cradle his balls, rubbing them ever so lightly. I use my other hand to reach behind his knee and motion for him to put that leg up, resting his foot on the balcony rail.

I release his long thick muscle and hold it up with my hand while I go under and tea bag his sac. Sucking, licking, and teasing him.

I lean my head back even further, and go under between his legs, placing my tongue on his anal area, and brushing it from the back to his balls. He grabs my head and pulls it in closer to his body. I stick the tip of my tongue in, and wiggle it.

Chapter 29

Greg

I closed my eyes and moaned her name, "Oh Susan what are you doing to me girl."

I had to ask that question she was blowing my mind. The feel of her lips and the wetness from her tongue was driving me crazy. The sounds coming from her was letting me know how much she was enjoying it too.

Now this was a woman that brought her "A" game in whatever she did. When I finally let go of her, she moved back and looked up at me with questions in her eyes.

"It's my turn now baby." I said as I took her by the hand and helped her up.

I pulled her close to me until we were chest to chest. I wrapped my hand around her hair and pulled her head back.

"Tonight I get to make love to you in my home where I had always planned. It started here in this place standing outside of that balcony when the idea of me making love to you first formed. I wanted to fuck you then but now I want to make love to you. Make your body crave only mine. I want to hear you calling my name begging me to cum inside of you and then and only then would I make you all mine."

I picked her up and walked to my bedroom and tossed her into the middle of my king size bed. She laid there looking up at me with the sexiest eyes I have ever seen. I opened her legs and kissed my way down until my lips touch the wetness between her thighs.

I took two fingers and opened her up and ran my tongue across her already harden clit. She moans as I started to suck and ran my teeth across it. When I pushed my fingers inside of her moistness her juices start running out.

My man was hard and all I wanted to do was bury myself deep inside of her, but I had to learn some self-control because what I want more than being deep inside of her was having her cumming inside my mouth,

So I closed my eyes while fingering her and let my tongue go to work.

Susan

My body started to shiver. My knees felt so weak. If I were standing I'd collapse right in place. His tongue was doing things to me only my heart could interpret. That's when I exploded... and I couldn't take any more, but he was on me and wasn't about to let up without giving me all of him.

His tongue and lips made its way up to mine, as he grabbed one of my legs he puts it on his shoulder and led it up to where my knee met my jaw.

Grabbing his stiff pleasure maker, he entered my wet jewel, sliding into me until he was snug. Then he stoked me ever so lovingly.

I followed his rhythm, and met him with every pump. When he went left I went right keeping my muscles tight around him.

We were in deep love. I could feel him pumping inside me like a heavy heartbeat after a morning jog. "Please don't ever stop." Was all I could think.

He released my leg and let it slide down his side; putting both arms around me... we rolled.

Now I'm on top, pushing my hands into his muscular chest and guiding myself upward. I began to ride him like he was the only man I had ever wanted in my life.

As I took all of him inside me I started to grind him with short pumps at a quick pace. I screamed out in between my moans. "This it."

After multiple orgasms, I felt another one building up and I knew that this one was going to be the big one.

Chapter 30

Greg

This time when she made love to me I could tell that she used all of her emotions. Her movements were different than before and I love it. I love her more each time that we made love.

I looked up at her and she had her head back with her mouth open as she rides me; her breasts bouncing up and down with her every move. She was beautiful.

I reached up and pulled her head down into a kiss. I just had to taste her sweet lips again. My hands moving through her hair and on down her back as I pumped in and out slowly. I wanted her to feel me everywhere, but importantly I wanted her to feel the power I had over her mind.

I can fuck her everyday but it want mean a damn thing if I can't get her mind as well. So that was my next goal I have her heart, body, and now I'm not stopping until she's not able to eat or sleep without thinking of me.

I felt her body starts to shake and I knew she was close to releasing again. I love to watch her as she cums, and it only makes me hit her spot faster and harder.

I felt her muscles tighten around my man. I bit down on my lip trying hard not to yell out. I had my arms wrapped around each of her shoulders and I started pushing her down harder and faster.

I felt her tighten around me all the way down into the bottom of my stomach. I knew I was close. My man got so hard I felt like I was about to explode like a volcano. I pumped and pumped until she was filled with my little soldiers. Shit she better watch out I might just hit the jack pot with this load.

Susan

Morning came quick as we greeted each other with a tight embrace and a passionate good morning kiss.

"Good morning my sweet sexy lady."

"Good morning my handsome officer." and a very good morning it is. I thought to myself.

If this is what being married to your soul mate is like then I'm all in, but now I started hating myself thinking about being with Tom, geesh, his poor wife and to think about I was sleeping with him. I never once thought twice about sleeping with a married man, but what if his wife believed that Tom was her soul mate? No I couldn't even think about that right now.

Greg and I both got up and headed for the shower.

"Hey love?"

"Yes Sue, darling?"

"No morning jog?"

"Not today, I have to be in the office early today. I have a mountain of paper work to do and the Captain says he needs to discuss some important matters with me. I can't imagine what that may be, although he may wanna chew my ass out for breaking protocol over you or my way of handling this case. My methods always seem a bit unorthodox, but I always get the job done".

I'm sure it's nothing at all being you survived on the force for as long as you have. It seems to me he should be used to you doing what it needs to get the job done."

"I'm sure Charles is just being Charles and all, always drinking that little bottle of Mylanta, says I give him reflux".

We both laugh as we jump in the shower. I was thinking about giving my man a good morning blowjob in the shower, but we have plenty of days of that coming. Besides I need to get a move on, I know there was going to be a board meeting today with the death of HK. I suppose the board will manage The Law Firm until they named the next CEO.

I was still getting dressed when Greg said, "Baby I gotta go, and I took the liberty of having your car brought here".

"Oh thank you baby I wanted to say something last night but thought better of it."

"Sweetie I never forget things like that. Plus I knew you needed a way around since I wasn't going to be around much today. I also left an extra set of house keys on the hook on the kitchen wall".

He walks over and kisses me.

"Enjoy your day my love".

"Ok Sweetie, you do the same."

Chapter 31

Greg

I walked into the station earlier then I like and Charles was already sitting in his office looking through paperwork. I walked in and took a seat. I already knew I was going to hear it, because not only was he my boss he was also my best friend. I was wandering who is going to confront me first.

"So you just going bring your happy ass in here and not say anything about the way you handled things yesterday?" Charles asked.

"Well I was going tell you.." Charles cut me off.

"You know what. I don't want to hear it, because it's only going to piss me off, but Greg that shit could have stopped this promotion you been working so hard for. Just what the hell were you thinking and before you say anything don't you tell me it was because of a piece of ass because you know better than that?"

I didn't know what to say but it made me mad that he thought of Susan as a piece of ass.

"Charles things' concerning Susan are different. I love her."

"You what?" Charles yelled. "Greg don't

fuck up your career over no damn woman. Plus you hardly know her."

I knew he was right on most of the things he said but Susan is good for me and she would never fuck up my career.

"Charles it's not like that with Susan and me. We are together now. I know I don't know everything I need to know about her, but what's important is that I know that she loves me as much as I love her. So if this happens to affect my promotion then there's always next year." I said as I dropped my reports of all the incidents that happened yesterday down on his desk.

Charles picked them up but he didn't look at it.

"It didn't affect nothing, you got your promotion Captain Brown congratulations." Charles stood up and held out his hand.

"Dammit Charles you had me going there for a minute." I said as I stood up taking his hand smiling. "You knew this all along why the hell you put me through all of that?"

"Because you needed it Greg that's why and promise me you won't go jumping off buildings for this Susan." I dropped his hand.

"I can't promise you that, but I'll damn sure try my friend,"

Charles handed me a new I.D. badge on my

way out of his office, and the first thing that came to mind was that I needed to call Susan and tell her the great news.

Susan

The board meeting was over and apparently I knew even less about HK then I thought. He already had someone highly recommended to head up The Law Firm. Mr. Peter Richardson was a silent partner and now he is the new CEO.

I made a mental note to do some homework on this character as well as HK. As the office cleared out to head over to the court house. My case had been reassigned because of my involvement which the board felt might compromise things.

I sat at my desk staring at one piece of evidence that never made it to police evidence room... the little flash drive. I pulled out my laptop and inserted it into the USB drive. *FEDERAL BUREAU OF INVESTIGATIONS* popped up on the screen. I hit enter and the screen read *"HIGHLY CONFIDENTIAL"*. Then it switched to 16 files and 8 videos.

I went through each file one by one, and just as I started the first video my cell went off. I jumped as it startled me, being on edge from the recent information I just discovered in the files. I looked at the caller ID and it was Greg.

"Hello sweetheart, how'd things go at the

office?"

"Well Charles dug into me deep, but Sue Baby... I did it, I made Captain".

"This calls for celebration so how about after work we meet up for dinner and drinks?"

"You're on Baby, hold on a sec. I have an incoming call".

Greg switches over as I look up at the screen and see someone shot to death in the first video. "OH MY GOD", I screamed out. "Who was that?" I put it on pause to go back to the beginning as Greg came back to the phone.

"Hello, hello Greg." There was silence.

Then he came in. "That was him Sue".

"Him who?"

"The man or mastermind behind this whole thing".

"He's calling you, why?"

"He started calling me when he wanted to trade, you for the key, but now."

"What sweetheart, what is it?"

"Well Baby don't be alarmed, but he wants you. You have something he wants".

"Oh no."

"What Sue, what is it that you have that he wants?"

"It's a flash drive sweetheart. I'm viewing it now and just saw a murder on it."

"What else is on it?"

"There are 16 files. Each file has a name on it and in each file is a list of contacts and illegal accounts of several events that date back over 20 years. I'm only on the first video, but let me email the contents of the drive to you and the only other person I can trust... Anthony."

"Sue, go on with your day as normal until we meet up tonight, and I'm putting two undercover detectives on you".

"They won't be visible to you, but they will be there and they're the best damn men I have".

"I love you and I will see you soon".

"I love you too Sweetheart."

I hung up and forward the flash drive email to both men. I went back to the first video and pressed play.

PEEK-A-BOO

(Sound Bite)

Two people become one / watching each other until dawn / didn't know it would be so much fun

Danger hiding around corners / then we become mourners Peek-A-Boo is the game that we play

Craving her ready to get laid / loving her was my only aid / it was like playing a hand of spades

Watching her was my only means/ with danger around every scene / she was like a drug something that I fiend

Two strangers in the night / loving each only by sight / on a stormy night / lighting flashing across the sky

That night we became one / Pee-A-Boo is the only song / happiness is around the corner

No more lonely nights / loving her feels so right/ two hearts that end up as one / our new life has just begun

BY: ATLANTAMOODY

Love at first sight / let's get it in right / watching
from the balcony / during the night

Under the moonlight / and lightning flashes / under
the canopy / where raindrops splashes

Visions of lashes / whips and French feathers /
peek-a-boo between two / nude in Trench
Leathers

Trend setters go getters / breaking the barriers /
aphrodisiac of the African carriers

The sheets will marry us / uniting as one / the
heat was spun / when intertwining begun

A hero's song sung / on how the love was captured
/ when two became sprung / and the love was
raptured

Hearts became plastered / on the souls within /
and what was separate from then / became whole
again

It's the story of a friend / when eyes met eyes /
and the joy of a surprise / that covered loneliness'
cries...

BY: POETICAL WORD PLAY

Coming

Soon

THE LYRICIST FIRM

PRESENTS

Love Or Death

By: Lynnett Fox

Love or Death: I closed my eyes and tried to sleep. The nightmares kept creeping in. He was hitting me with relentless force. He wouldn't stop. Would I live through this? Christina "Wada" Thomas thought she had met the perfect vato when she met Marco, little did she know that her knight would take her on a dark and twisted road of drug abuse. The final showdown being when he tried to get her into prostitution. We take a journey through Weda's Vida Loca and the climax being when she lives through The Day of the Dead or does she? Did her path lead to Love or Death?

Little Girl Lost : Susie comes home to find her house empty. What happened to her mother and little brother? Had they left her and moved somewhere else? Susie has always been the invisble one now it seems like she really is.

Its been mouths that Sandy has been searching for her missing daughter. Will she find her in time? What happens when a little girl becomes lost?

Writersblock Publications Presents

JUSTIFIED MEANS TO THE END

BY: QUAMEEK KALEPH

Justified Means To The End: The everyday complex struggles of Mik'hail Drayton. An inner city youth raised in the cold streets of Savannah, GA criminal underworld as a product of his environment. Through his trials and tribulations he takes an oath to uplift his people and learns the truth about "Freedom of Choice". In the game of life and death, he learns that stakes are high and bets are eternal. Mik'hail must choose between his free-will and will to be free. Either way he must learn that those who master the game know and understand that only the End can Justify the Means.

WRITERSBLOCK
PUBLICATIONS

Presents

THE HAUNTING OF
CHRISTINA
ROCKWELL

By: Veronica Meek

The Haunting Of Christina Rockwell: After the death of Christina's mother her father decided it was best that they move back to his hometown. Once she arrived there Christina saw that they were out in the middle of nowhere in a small country town. She wasn't happy about the move but when the visited the house for the first time Christina came face to face with a ghost. Now she is going to try everything in her power to find out who this ghost is and why she is trapped inside their country home.

The Hitman's Dauther's: The Hitman's Daughters
tell a story of many interesting people living in
the streets of Atlanta, GA. Many hard times,
family secrets, stuggles, and troubles center one
of the main characters, Star. Join us as we all
learn more about Star, Muffin, Red. Tracey,
Stacy, Rick, and Tony as they battle this life.

This is E book only…

http://www.snackphood.com/store/product.php?i
d_product=34

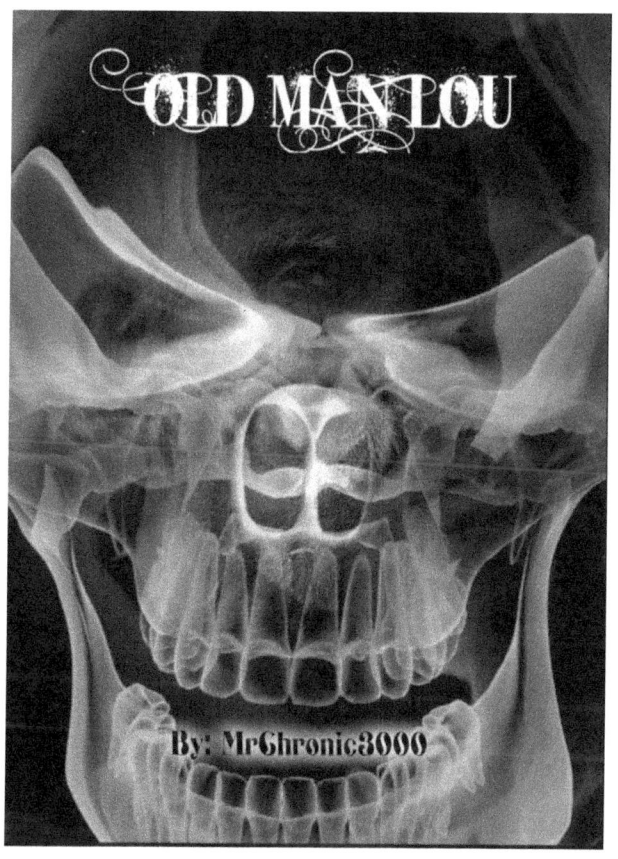

OLD MAN LOU

By: MrChronic3000

Lou was a well-known figure in his neighborhood. He had everything going for him. Then one day news spreads of Lou's suicide. He allegedly shot his self with a .38.Only problem is Lou didn't own a .38. Detective Danny Westfield was Lou's young protégé and husband to Lou's daughter. One day Danny gets word that Lou's Death was not a suicide. Det. Westfield begins a journey for answers. The more he digs the more he finds out that this case is bigger than Lou. No one can be trusted. Everyone is a suspect. Join Det. Westfield on his journey for answers.

Life for me has been a constant battle of ups
and downs .Yet, I am still able to call myself
blessed and highly favored .Through all the
troubles I have faced, one thing has never
changed. That is the fact that my savior
Jesus Christ has never allowed me to face
them alone. In the mist of every storm, i
have been able to focus on the silver lining
surrounding the black clouds that seem to
follow me.

www.ingramcontent.com/pod-product-compliance
Lightning Source LLC
Chambersburg PA
CBHW051503170626
46811CB00002B/625